To Rhy[illegible]
I learn[illegible]
I do too [illegible]
your swing!

Best Regards,

THE SAGA OF JOE MONK

Jim Snyder

"The Greatest Golfer of Olive Chapel"

P.S. I understand that
your mother is even
better than you –
she is a great
lady in all respects

James E. Snyder, Jr.

Universal Publishers • USA • 2000
ISBN: 1-58112-729-4

Front cover art by Chip Holton, Lexington, NC
Back cover photograph by Tommy Sink, Lexington, NC

DEDICATION
to
William Snyder Lancaster
our grandson

IN MEMORY
of
Elvis and Pearl

IN HONOR
of
My Aunt Bea

OTHER BOOKS BY AUTHOR

Take Counsel, "A Lawyer Discusses Law and Life," Universal Publishing Company, 2000

A Lawyer Prays God's Will for His Clients, Universal Publishing Company, 2000

Snyder North Carolina Automobile Insurance Law, The Harrison Company Publishers, Suwanee, Georgia, Third Edition, 1999

Snyder North Carolina Corporation Law and Practice, The Harrison Company Publishers, Suwanee, Georgia, Third Edition, 2000

Snyder North Carolina Corporation Law and Practice Forms, The Harrison Company Publishers, Suwanee, Georgia, Third Edition, 1999

North Carolina Automobile Insurance Law, The Harrison Company Publishers, Norcross, Georgia, Second Edition, 1994

Snyder North Carolina Corporation Law and Practice, The Harrison Company Publishers, Norcross, Georgia, Second Edition, 1995

Snyder North Carolina Corporation Law and Practice Forms, The Harrison Company Publishers, Norcross, Georgia, Second Edition, 1995

North Carolina Automobile Insurance Law, The Harrison Company Publishers, Norcross, Georgia, First Edition, 1991

Snyder North Carolina Corporation Law and Practice, The Harrison Company Publishers, Norcross, Georgia, First Edition, 1991

Snyder North Carolina Corporation Law and Practice Forms, The Harrison Company Publishers, Norcross, Georgia, First Edition, 1990

TABLE OF CONTENTS

PREFACE

In the nineteen thirties and forties two highways crossed the United States from the north to the south and from the east to the west or from the south to the north or the west to the east, U.S. Highways 1 and sixty four respectively. They crossed in Raleigh, the capitol city, linking golfers to each other and courses to courses, the poles of Highway 1, MacKenzie's Oakley course near Boston and his Augusta course in Georgia, and the poles of Highway sixty four, Carmel and Pebble Beach to the west and to the east, Pinehurst and Number 2; and, near the juncture of these great ribbons of transportation, Olive Chapel, where Joe Monk lived, with Pinehurst to the south and Wake Forest to the north, where Joe's challenger would learn.

Sixty-four meandered eastward through what was soon to be the world's greatest nation and her heart cities of Tucson and Albuquerque and Dallas and Little Rock and Memphis and Nashville then Asheville, now Mocksville, then across the Yadkin River to Davidson's capitol city of Lexington, where we live, then on eastward to Papa's house in Olive Chapel and the land of Joe Monk, the greatest golfer, and of Mr. Elvis and Miss Pearl.

Mr. Elvis and Miss Pearl were the oldest in their respective homes, he being reared with Grandpa At and Miss Liza one mile west of New Hill on Highway 1 and she a mile farther to the west, nearer to the chapel, with her parents Grandpa Tody and Grandma Nelia, the Goodwins. And after Elvis married Pearl, his two brothers Humie and Emmet, being impressed with the Goodwin genetic pool, reached in and pulled out Aunt Susie and Aunt Minnie to complete not only the potential for a plethora of double first cousins but also a continuation of contiguous Olive-Goodwin farms from Highway 1 to sixty four. Mr. Elvis was tall and lean with a face of the Spanish and the English, a head more rectangular than any other in the Carolinas, chocolate brown eyes, pencil straight nose and a mouth not unlike the one more famous who would follow, named similarly; a voice and a manner of articulation that would have made the southern legislative triumvirate of Holland, Helms and Thurman gush with envy and a man who always was at the back door to welcome and who never allowed a visitor to leave without "seein him out," standing there watching the guest back up the old dirt road; and, she, would later be the oldest living alumna of Meredith College, the Baptist women's college, sister to Wake Forest, and for a while a school teacher at New Hill before accepting the southern woman's birthright, possession and control of a farm and of every living being and creature on it, her hair always in a bun and usually partially strewn, her art was for cooking and her artistry her children, all broad shouldered and big smiling. Like Joe Monk, her farm her world and it and those things which comprised it being the entry point and the exit for seeds and harvest and all the cousins and kin who made up this world of richness and wood smoke and cream and honey and sausage that only Papa could make on the day of the killings when the hogs hanged by their heels and in futility ran for their lives as if running from the stars and the fire of the sun. Life and death co-existed in the world of Elvis and Pearl and all the Olives of Olive Chapel, each farm state autonomous, she the queen, he the king and on each all others dependent, those twenty to thirty tenants, all black who respected each other and the queen and the king no less and they them, but of all those creatures within this state there was only one of full strength, she, the queen, and on sister farms her sisters and all the rest who encouraged, cajoled, swatted flies, beheaded chickens, feed thirty, three times a day, and was a woman too and a lady and a lover - for survival was important, they the last true people of the land, for they knew fullwell or sensed that the future would be different; that the children would never return to the farm; that they would move to town in its generic and literal sense, but would always return with the grandchildren to play in the barns, around the ponds and even in the low grounds and maybe to work or to play at working and certainly to work at playing, black boys and white boys, dreaming together by the cool stream that aimlessly was there in the low grounds below the tenant house where Joe Monk lived and played - above it all.

James E. Snyder, Jr.
Lexington, N.C.
April   2000

CHAPTER ONE

GOING BACK TO OLIVE CHAPEL

Spring, Two Thousand Ten

"Papa, why are we going to Olive Chapel?"

"For many years I have felt that this day would come - that I would journey with you, my grandchild, back to my grandfather's farm, there to relive with you the story of Joe Monk, the greatest golfer of Olive Chapel; and, for that matter, undeniably the greatest black golfer of all times and potentially the greatest golfer of any time. To walk again over the fields where Joe practiced as a boy, once more to experience the sights and sounds of the farm where I too lived so many exciting days as a boy working in tobacco, to help you feel and understand something of the magic of Olive Chapel and its blessed people and to give you some sense of your own history and mine which has been quite magically intertwined with one of golf's unknown and forgotten legends will be for me a final and fulfilling experience. But, today you are going to learn about more than tobacco, the sweet smell of my grandmother's kitchen and of Joe Monk, I am going to tell you of the essence of golf as known only to Joe; because, you see, I believe that he had discovered the answer, by that I mean the last and final lesson of golf, which can unlock in any person who knows and understands, the ability from that time on to propel a golf ball within feet of the intended goal. This very day you will know and understand the secret of grooving an absolutely repetitive, consistent, world class swing. But the answer and the secret is not in a sentence; it is in a story; it is not in a lesson, but in several; and, it cannot be absorbed and applied without an appreciation of the sum of its parts: each lesson must be heard, and understood before the final lesson can be inserted into the spirit of the golfer to unlock the champion that's within him."

"Papa, how long is all this going to take? You know that Mimi expects us home for supper."

"Ah, yes . . . but, your grandmother learned long ago . . . that golfers always are late for supper."

Olive Chapel, a quiet tobacco farming community of God's sweetest people, lies just along U.S. Highway 1 in Carolina (northern); amazingly and consistently along that same venerable traffic way lies the village of Pinehurst, forty miles to the south, the incubator, preserver and center of American golf, final home and canvas of golf's greatest artist,

2

Donald Ross, and his masterpiece, Number 2; and, equidistant to the north along that same roadway, nestled among two hundred year old magnolias, is the village of Wake Forest, birthplace of golf's greatest collegiate juggernaut and alma mater of a young golfer arrived from Columbus, Ohio, to that old Baptist campus; and, far to the south sits golf's flower along that same road, Augusta National created by the Yorkshireman, Alister MacKenzie, where a tournament evolved which was to supplant the North and South Amateur and the North and South Open in Pinehurst as the first breath of Spring; then, finally and remarkably far to the north Highway 1 ends at Oakley, MacKenzie's other course, in Watertown, near Boston, the course from whence James Tufts departed to create the village of Pinehurst and to which he returned to bring with him its pro, Donald Ross, a Freemason, born of Scotland in Dornoch. These places, these people, this highway and the game of golf so amazingly were interconnected and one day would combine to nourish, develop and propel golf's two greatest toward the epic match and the final lesson.

"Papa, who was Joe Monk?"

"My grandfather, Elvis Elisha Olive, and my grandmother, who we called Grandmommie, were such good people. When I stayed with them during summers I first was allowed to drive the mule sleds between the rows that carried the tobacco from the fields to the looping tables. My heart would leap at daybreak when hearing the jingle of the harnesses and the sound of the wooden sleds across the sandy, rocky Wake County soil. On the farm lived many tenant farmers all of whom were black. We all worked together from sun-up to sun-down effectively moving Carolina's cash crop to market. The farm was a family: black people and white people, working hard, eating well and sleeping the sleep of the dead. But, Joe Monk was different. He had a small bed in the

3

unpainted curtilage building just in back of the main house. On Sunday afternoons I would wander into that building and find old hidden secret treasures and would go over to the small dusty window under which was Joe's bed, behind the bags of feed in brown tow sacks with more privacy provided by an old dresser and stacked boxes with nothing in them.

"One day right before supper I was standing in the dirt roadway with the main house to my left and the milk barn to my right. Grandmommie came to the back door and yelled across my head to my uncle, 'James, Joe Monk has drunk more perfume, and he looks like he's going to die!' My uncle, a man's man and a good man, without malice and without prejudice but as a matter of resolute exasperation hollered back across my head, 'Mama . . . just let him die!'

"I never forgot the empathy, the wonderment, and the frustration that I felt when those words were spoken, words not of cruelty but of real life existence on a beautiful tobacco farm in the mid nineteen fifties. After supper that night, while Papa and I were walking through the cool darkness checking the fires in the tobacco barns - just as we had exited the barn closest to the fish pond, while deep groans of the many bullfrogs echoed through the hollow and down over the dam to the five curing barns surrounding a yard, I summonsed the courage to ask my mother's father to tell me about this special man, who slept closest the big house, under the dusty window, in semi-privacy, and who obviously was so different and so torn. Papa removed his well-chewed hickory snuff stick from his firmly set and sharply squared southern jaw, and in Helmsian resonant voice developed from generations of proud southern men, in a tone so deep that his words flowed directly to the ground and lay there in the dark grass, and he said, 'Let's go to the house.' There we sat, just he and I, in that room with the large eating table clothed in slick flowered oil cloth and six high back chairs, where he and Grandmommie lived all those years before

4

the fire and to which the entire extended family would gravitate to enjoy the many feasts on Sundays, there under the single light from the cord through the ceiling we sat into the warm summer night, and he told me the story of Joe Monk while the sounds of Grandpa Tody's pendulum clock ebbed and flowed from the mantel over the old hearth where your great grandmother was rocked and by which I had been measured to determine if sufficient stature had been reached to receive my first pony; into the night and into the morning I only listened, and I learned of the saga of Joe Monk - and so shall you."

"Papa are we there yet?"

"No but we're getting there, at least half way to Asheboro."

"Are we going to the big mountains."

"No, the Blue Ridge are far behind us. These are the Uwharries, the oldest mountains in the world, now worn rather small. All my life I had heard that these hills were old, we'll come camping here someday. Two hundred million years ago when the continents were all stuck together and then before that when they sank under the sea, there was one tip of land visible for all to see which was the highest of these mountains - which then were lofty - but they've been weathered and shaped by the wind and the rain. They deserve our respect because they're old, and they have survived and they can teach us a good deal."

"Teach us?"

"Remember that you don't need vocal chords to be a teacher or a brain or a degree - you need only ears and the mind and the attention of students who observe and receive information from things that have lasted and survived. The mountains and the course will teach you far more than any

5

professional or even a grandfather. Watch and listen what the course and the land have to say and never never fight them - become a part of them, and they all will become a part of you. You see it's about gravity, the force that sticks it all together: it will bring the ball down to earth at a certain time and in a certain way and then will pull the ball to one spot or the other against the sloop of the land; and, that's about it - the ball will fall and roll against the sloop of the land in response to the force applied at the beginning and consistent with the friction between the ball and the grass. Believe me, your grandfather tends to forget these things. But, if you forget the first rule of golf you'll be fighting God's nature and the forces within it, and you'll never be a champion, and you'll never pull from our favorite game the satisfaction that it wants to give to us all."

CHAPTER TWO

HIT A ROCK AND RABBIT'S TAIL

Autumn, Nineteen Forty One

Crack! . . . Crack! . . . Crack! . . .

A long dirt road from the main highway flowed slightly downward a well struck driver's length to the main house and by it on the left; the milk barn on the right and then down even more a three iron and up a rise and then to the right and slightly downward the length of a shortish par four to the main tenant house perched on a bluff above the low grounds, a green area of sandy soil, flooded each decade by an otherwise quiet creek;

7

and, the road then small and flat through the expansive fields beyond which was a line of trees, rather swampy-like, from which I shied, the limits of the farm and a place of uncertainly; these low grounds, which every farm has, because every farm has a creek and a pond or ponds, around and in which cows graze during the day because it's cool before returning up that long winding fence line over hard rocky ground, over the dam of the cow pond into which flowed the rich sediment from the small pasture adjacent to the milk barn across from the main house; that pasture always was bright green with healthy grass and dark black of manure troddened dirt leading into the barn - all these things smelled good, but better in the evening after steamy hot afternoons.

A ten year old black boy lived in this world, and it was all the world he needed, with more adventure and work and hot biscuits and crayfish and horse flies and farm activity that would make any young boy's mind swell with excitement, like a sailor on a ship - this land was all there was.

He had one pair of pants, probably once dark blue, now the color of the earth, rolled to just below his knees, and two shirts, winter and summer, and one pair of shoes, winter. With nine siblings, his father, Mr. Benny, and his grandmother, Ursula, Joe lived in the tenant house, overlooking his own course, the holes of which changed each day to fit his swing pattern, a course which although flat in reality dived and rose and dog-legged to conform with his own imagination. He fit those small black hands around his own tobacco stick, carefully selected from the stack and now well worn at both ends from a thousand daily swings at wondrous targets and colored flags, under gusty winds and on to accomplished championships, and he was happy.

Crack! . . . Crack! . . . Crack! . . .

The small white smooth river pebbles, indigenous to Olive Chapel, worn and polished by millions of years of elements, a one piece ball without balata or surlyn or lithium or even gutta purcha hide; those small stones, also the color of Joe Monk's trousers, cracked from the larger end of Joe's tobacco stick with one purpose toward one goal - a crow carelessly and heedlessly flying within Joe Monk's reach only for its course necessarily to be averted by a missile intended to warn but not to harm - rabbits, as well, venturing into range, having their white tails dusted, not still, but while on the run, by Joe's perfectly aimed and precisely intended missiles. Yes, he was that good - he never harmed, but he always warned; and, not one hopping/flying creature lost his life to this golfer.

This youngest of swings, congenitally perfect, flowed low straight and away - then through, then down through to high finish with the rhythm on the low grounds which was the rhythm of creation, he never thinking how - only where.

But, the swing, in reality, was a grip - a grip like no others, even at this age, a grip with no variance, with a life of its own as if each hand had a brain with synapses extending to the depths of that stick to its pronounced end resulting in unparalleled stick-head speed and that Crack! - that unwavering consistent sound trumpeting to the boy's brain that his swing was accomplished and its purpose completed - not a boy's grip, but a man's grip, not as holding a small bird but instead as holding a steel hammer, the grip of a blacksmith, the grip of a warrior unsheathing his sword.

No one taught Joe Monk to hold the stick lightly, loosely, gently, lovingly - do that and a tobacco stick will reward you with splinters; it will slip, twist and contort and sting and bite - so that stick was his first teacher. Joe Monk's grip was firm and tight and strong, the only contact with his inanimate extension fully in both hands, not his fingers, unlike all other golfers - save one, but still golf's only true prodigy.

There, just before sunset every evening he played: you see, he never practiced; it always was play - and always with

9

a full stomach. Something everyone in Olive Chapel knew was that it was better to be poor with one pair of pants and to eat soft biscuits mixed from hog lard and chicken fried in it, with milk gravy, cooked sugared apples and mixed beans and corn boiled in hog meat with tea so sweet that sugar formed averations like heat waves rising always upward like serpents in the sea, than to live on Hillsborough Street in Raleigh with twenty suits eating dietary supplements and skimmed everything. After three pieces of apple pie he would pop in a score more biscuits, each round, small, warm and still smelling of buttermilk and dough, just to fill up the empty spaces and wash it all down with one more tall ball jar glass of that sweet nectar of the gods, sweet tea taxed from the mother country.

Joe never knew his mother. She was white, most thought; but, we'll get to that later.

"Joe Monk! boy, git up to dis house. Ah prays ever night dat God, the Lord Almighty, 'ul stop a' makin all dem rocks - or better yet, that you'll finally hit 'em all."

"Granny, I'm commin" his soft low voice echoing through the now cooling low grounds as Joe determinedly drove his two iron through the ball causing it to sail high with the slightest draw to an elevated green, bounce once to the right and land three feet under the eighteenth at Number 2, a place in his mind's eye, but where he had been before. Joe never putted in the low grounds because he always hit his rocks so close. That three-footer was a gimmie - as were all his putts. As he entered the old back plank hinged door into the kitchen still hot from the wood stove, over to the low seated chair beside the fire, he laid his stick at the mantle, washed his face, hands and feet in the bucket of cold well water and crawled under his cover on his bed in the loft.

"Joe, did ah heah yoe little self jump in dat bed wift aught yoe prayas?"

"Yes, ma'am." And Joe's knees met the floor, his

Belefontish profile casting a shadow from the yellow fire below onto the ceiling of the loft, this young player bowing before the Creator of the low grounds who formed the rocks before Joe was born.

That same night in Columbus, far to the north, Beacon Smead also put his prodigy to bed. The young pro's son each night, every night, smoothed the transition from consciousness to unconsciousness by re-living and re-playing the day's shots - of others - as he caddied for them and later in the evening his own - along and among the western green rolling hills of Ohio; yet, his shots had not been pure, and he was worried. Maybe it was the hands - tomorrow he would push then forward and up; certainly that would preset the clubhead to move more to the inside with the backswing - but then he pictured in his mind's eye, as he nearly drifted into sleep, and he wondered, about his left arm and the elbow - should he preset it, the elbow, to the target to his left or even more under so as to lock his left arm more rigidly to prevent its collapse, as it inevitably collapsed, but only slightly with each swing. That's it - tomorrow - high hands forward with elbow facing target; those would be his swing keys.

The world, his only world and a big enough world was just awakening, the sky barely visible to the east and beyond the Harris place, the tobacco fields lay awaiting, dripping with morning dew surrounding the pond; and, up beyond that massive oak which would shade the table of tobacco from the fields and around it on each side the handers and loopers, three leaves at a time, their hands growing stickier with black tobacco tar; and, the rhythmic hoofbeats and harness sounds of the large black beasts, strong and unpredictable, the mules with primers on their backs moving to the east back up the road by the big house on the right to the Harris place, across the main road to hitch to the sleds, which slid on sandy soil and not on ice or snow but in sweltering weather, not freezing, which were made of rough timber along which were hung curtains of canvas, these sleds pulled through the rows and piloted by Joe, starting and stopping at the commands of the primers, with Joe perched astride the back of the sleds on their sides that did not collapse, to accept the bundles of the green wet crop which years in the future would be converted by fire to smoke to enter the lungs of humanity around the world and do what only tobacco smoke can do. The biscuits had been hot and the eggs runny and the ham so salty that Joe's lips would taste of it for hours later until the salt of his own body replaced it to be washed away by water from the gourd cup.

"Joe, thar's Mr. James . . . and . . . he's got wift 'm little Jimmy Olive," screeched Miss Ursula from her hot kitchen.

And Joe leaped from the house and the porch over the dogs and with thirty other tenant workers sat around the trailer pulled by the tractor, sixty legs dangling all around, all without shoes as the tractor went slightly down and then up by the milk barn on the left and the big house on the right across the main road through the winding path and the thick heart pine which grew only along that unique place where millennia ago the ocean lapped its waves over the sandhills to this crescent area which at one time was the shore of the continent, these thick oak-like pines darting a full nine iron into the air and common only to this area and to Augusta. Then three barns the primers picked, just the leaves slightly tan and yellow nearest the bottom of the stalk, their long black powerful fingers snapping

12

each leaf discernibly ripe not by vision but by the pressure of the appendage against the stalk, causing it to give way and to snap, with the thousands of snaps throughout the day combined with the sound of the sled over hard rocky ground as the sun was relentless. It would not be until dark that the field hands and Joe returned to the community of barns surrounding a yard behind the big house, and there the primers' legs stretched and toes curled around timbers high in the barns stacking the money crop now hanging from sticks from barn's top to its bottom; and, after twelve hours in the field and two in the barn, these strong working people, both white and black, walked to their houses to bath, eat and sleep and to rise in the morning and do it again, except some who must sleep in the sleds by the barns all night tending the fires that cooked the crop that would later burn providing smoke for men's lungs or sweet juice in their mouths to be spit on the ground.

The heat of summer had escaped heavenward leaving autumn's hues which fell earthward. Now the morning was cold and clear; all farming had stopped for two months as the land rested and froze. Joe remembered that morning. When Miss Ursula sat him on a stool in the back of Miss Pearl's cupboard and told him to shush, for where there always had been laughter, Joe heard sobbing, which signaled the death of a child as Mr. Elvis moved slowly by to walk the farm and weep alone. He heard the women gathering strength from the loss of a grandson, James' boy, who yesterday had such a round healthy face, the promise to carry on the farm, and today because of a prescription reaction, would no longer sit in Miss Pearl's kitchen eating the dough dipped in the flour; and, the phone rang, our ring - two longs and a short - was she Frances or Bea or Jeanette, and Miss Pearl must tell the girls that we all were one fewer in number; and, the life of the farm and the death of the farm was real, as they lived it and swallowed it; but, again that spring sewed seed - but for a time all stood still; and, as he approached the low grounds Mr. Elvis could hear the child's laughter and then his scream as he ran from the packhouse, the month before, announcing to all that the "bacca is burning," a half a year's crop had been neatly looped and sorted and tied, its gold color belying the worth of the labor which brought it to harvest to sell in the autumn for enough to pay off the loan and to buy more seed to renew the cycle which now seemed without purpose or method or end or reward; the flames of the packhouse too the crops color; and, then, to the west, he spotted the gap in the trees where the sun set each night by the chapel of the Olives where their faith was established and maintained and which now seemed uncertain, at least for a moment; but, then a resolute prayer and a sigh and the crying was ended and as he returned to Pearl's kitchen, Joe seemed to realize that healing had sprung by his home in the low grounds, and he dozed and remembered his friend now departed. And around the fire the others gathered; it had taken their crop but now its orange embers and warm glow and crackles were giving, not taking to all those who looked in its healing and warmth; and, they would endure.

"Now, you must remember that my grandfather was no golfer, he was a farmer. But, a farmer loves the land, the soil, the wind, the rain, the sunshine, the fresh green grass in the spring and the dryness of the summer, the flowering of the trees in April and the colorful demise of each leaf in October, with the harvest and with the return of coolness. But as you grow

14

older you'll increasingly find yourself going out to the only farms that are left, the courses. There you'll watch the grass grow in the spring and grow dormant in the winter, you'll cross streams and tramp under the winds and through thickets and swamps in search of something white and round; you'll throw grass in the air and listen for the breeze, and you'll farm the only way a golfer can farm. As you well can smell and swing and listen and struggle to appreciate the truth of your swing, there will be a parallel emotional fruition within the secret of the perpetuation of that swing, and by diligence and pure dedication of thought you can learn and remember and perpetuate your best swing and more importantly that progression will parallel your understanding of you."

"Sir? . . ."

"You see, your great, great grandfather, Mr. Elvis, never needed golf; but you will. On a farm there is life and death and wind and rain. As a business person or a professional you won't see calves born and eggs laid; in your office you'll find no breezes and learn nothing of the philosophy of the earth and emotional release and control; and, that is why God made golf.

"Now, all this is what made Joe Monk so great: he was a farmer and a golfer, and I will challenge any man or woman to name more than five who were both. One does not beget the other, each has what the other has; therefore, each feels no magnetic opposite pole or pull to the other. Golf will keep your spirit alive."

CHAPTER THREE

PINEHURST

Winter, Nineteen Thirty Six

"Papa, are we there yet?"

"Someday I want to take you to Carmel, California, seventeen mile drive, Pebble Beach, Spy Glass Hill, Cypress Point, where soft rolling hills by the ocean are cooled by the fog of Monterey Bay, the lovely streets shaded by pines, golf's western heaven. But, there is a better place - a purer place - a place Carmellish but far better - a place as soft and lovely, as gentle and nostalgic as Olive Chapel, a place where the scent of pine trees, long leafed, join with that of magnolias and azaleas,

16

thick with hollies and cedars. Every growing vegetation in Pinehurst is evergreen, with green glossy leaves more striking in winter than in summer because of contrast with dormant bermuda. This village of Pinehurst, with nineteenth century houses and dirt sidewalks and inns called The Magnolia and The Holly and the grand hotel, The Carolina, with huge veranda leading to side yards of rolled greens where you putt and within that grand central columned promenade the dining hall, where the southern cuisine is unparalleled, served primarily to northern folk at this island resort with no water surrounded by barren sand hills which just happen to crest at precise yardages of one hundred, two hundred and three hundred, where the ocean once lapped as at Augusta, and as at Oakley, where Donald Ross had but to clear away the brush and honor his partnership with the Creator by understatedly sowing grass and with mule pans leveling greens leading from and to the Pinehurst Country Club, whose brick veranda crescents the eighteenth green and beyond golf's first practice tee, its stuccoed cream yellow walls and arched green columns beckoning weary golfers to sit for a while under fans which circle and interrupt the light casting rotating shadows on worn brick steps chiseled and autographed by the cleats of Jones, Snead, Nelson, Lema, Palmer and Nicholas, the home of the North and South Amateur, the North and South Open and the home of golf's greatest architect's greatest course. The venerable, the revered, the natural, the incomparable Number 2 which is so stunningly beautiful and green that one's breath is taken when the course sings and breaths through its gills of long leaf pine as a soft southern air carries the village church chimes over this Rossian paradise."

It was here that Mr. Benny was born and where he, as a young boy worked the mules for Mr. Ross on Number 2. Before that he had been the yard boy for Mr. Tufts who developed this yankee village, this New England Village at the one spot, the one unique spot closest to the North that would provide a pleasant winter retreat for the wealthy northern industrialists along Highway 1.

Mr. Benny had been a striking, willowy, strong six footer with long delicate hands which with a twitch of the reins could send a signal to a mule's lips causing the beast to complete the dream of Mr. Ross by finally sculpting what already was there. Word was that Mr. Benny fell in love with one of the foreman's daughters, Maggie Kelly, a hanging offense back in those days in the South. She had come down with her family from Waltham, in New England with her father who was building the clubhouse; she was lonely, precocious, and frisky - and without prejudice, and she appreciated the quick smile the fast wit and the strong features of Benny Monk. One warm summer night hidden by the impenetrable rows of those unique beautiful pine brows, at a place so lovely and enchanting that remarkably it would be the very spot on which would be built the Number Five green of the Number 2 course, the greatest of holes on the greatest of courses - it was there that a child was conceived and who, to avoid scandal, had to be forfeited by his mother in favor of his father, a child who later would be called Joe. After the child was born in Aberdeen, a distraught, broken hearted mother, without choice, was spirited back to Massachusetts by her parents leaving this mule man and their son at Pinehurst.

During these years Donald Ross was completing Pinehurst Number Four, but all the while he tinkered with Number 2. Mr. Benny and Joe lived with several families there and sometimes were required to live as far away as Candor and to commute back to the village of the rich. Many

18

days Joe would go with his father and be relegated to fill his days watching the mule teams work their magic on the land.

The courses at Pinehurst are contiguous. The number one holes of the original four courses extended from the clubhouse and ended at the clubhouse. Golf was everywhere and little Joe was too. As a little boy he became like a vapor amongst the courses, always seeing but never seen, dodging among the hollies and the cedars and the azaleas as the rich people from the north with their strong caddies "farmed" the land. Joe was mesmerized by the beautiful gleaming white balls on the tightly mown contoured bermuda; and the sound of the persimmon polished wood compressing those beautiful white balls. But more people played there than the rich and the unaccomplished golfer. Pinehurst soon became a mecca for the greatest of the greats, and Joe saw them all and learned from them all and mimicked them all. He learned that an old dogwood tree root formed a mallet-like club. At first he hit pine cones, then rocks, then from time to time balls of the wealthy that were hit but not found or even searched.

At the age of seven Mr. Benny told his boy about The Tournament. He promised to take him - but he couldn't be there, that is, he could go but not be seen. The only black folks at Pinehurst in the nineteen thirties were working black folks. Joe watched Bobby Jones play Gene Sarazen. He saw Walter Hagan go head-to-head with Lloyd Mangrum. They all swung differently. They all swung viciously. They all swung with grace and uniqueness and abandon. Joe could copy anybody doing anything, but he never copied their swings. He only stood and observed, and then he swung. Not only did Joe love golf, he loved the people's clothes - the brown and white shoes of the men, the knickers, the long sleeved white shirts with colorful ties and the slicked back hair so common in the thirties.

The story goes that there are some holes that Donald

Ross left pretty much to Mr. Benny to mold and sculpt as he desired. During the years that they worked together Mr. Benny would later tell of the conversations that they had. In one of those conversations while completing the eleventh hole on Number Four the great architect and his man stood looking over the expanse of land before them.

"Mr. Donald, I see this hole moving to the right with the green right up there beyond the highest hillcrest."

"Benny, Benny, Benny, ye've been with me long enuf to know what we ar abut."

"What's that Mr. Donald?"

"Me challenge as a golf architect is not just to build gulf carses. Me job is to create an experience o the body and o mind and spirit, and if those three elements do nut cum together on this gulf carse on every hole, and on every shut on every hole, then I have failed both me benefactor and me Creator. It's not me job to try to trick the gulfer; it's me job to present to the gulfer what's thar, nothing more - nothing less. It's not me job to create hidden hazards, perilous stances and impossible dilemmas. When a gulfer plays me carse, he knows what to expect! Now, he should no expect to hit a ball on a green or near a green without being challenged. A green should no be like the inside of a spoon - but it's top, with each corner turning downward enabling the green to drain and breath while fairly challenging the gulfer to pitch, chip and putt frum uf the green. And, Joe, I do no believe in carses that are overly long, greens that are overly large or severely bunkered. The natural flow o the land takes care o ul these problems."

"Mr. Donald, you build golf courses. What about the . . .?"

"Benny, if I could impart anything to the gulfer it would be this: the carse creates the game and within the layout of the carse is the secret to conquering that carse. The land is flat or hilly; the green is course or even and slopes from the left to the right or to the front or the back; the earth is sandy or like clay or is black and soft; the air is by the surf or in the hills and is warm or is cold; and, the hole is to the green's left or the right or the front, or the back; yet, Benny, I see these gulfers come ut and hit a ball like they are hitting off a living rum carpet. I want to stop 'em and shake 'em and tell 'em to take a minute to thank Godt for the creation that's before 'em and to luk at what ye and I and He have dun and to consider the elements and then to make a plan far each shut. Each shut must be the result no uf thought as much as perception and feel leading to an intended swing and ball trajectory that matches and flows with the land and grass and the air and the temperature and the direction of the hole. Whether the gulfer hits the ball intendedly low or high or with a draw or a fade or even with a hook or a slice from time to time, he should no fight his swing or our carse. Benny, the essence o the game is the carse, and each carse is different so each swing o each club and each shut entirely is different from any other swing and shut ever made by the gulfer; therefar, each swing is one of life's unique experiences, and it must be savored and experienced after it has been nurtured and perceived; and, if done in that manner, the results will be satisfactory because they will culminate from the creation of the elements and the nature of the creature striking the ball and not in opposition to 'em. Benny? I may be going too far har - do you play gulf?"

"No, sir, Mr. Donald, I'm a farmer."

Shortly after Benny Monk's conversation with golf's greatest architect Mr. Ross was called to build courses up and down the eastern coast to the left and right of Highway 1, and Benny and Joe felt a call home back to the Olive farm.

"Papa, are we there yet?"

"No, we're about half way; this is Siler City."

"Like in Andy and Barny and Aunt Bea?"

"Why, yes, as a matter of fact, the real Aunt Bea or the lady who played Aunt Bea, after they made all of those programs, came back to live and die in Siler City, and as luck would have it, her lawyer was a classmate of mine, one J. Samuel Williams, Esquire. Sam was a - well, Sam always had a grin on his face. He's played football at North Carolina and was just a big loveable fellow . . . Sam sat in front of me in law school, and one day in our constitutional law class, Dr. Devine, who we called "foggy" because word was, he drove off from a filling station and left his family before realizing the error of his ways, called on Sam. Now, Sam was a bit nervous in class when called on; but I, sitting directly behind him whispered for him to settle down, and things would be fine. Well, Foggy Devine asked Sam a question, and I said 'yes' and Sam said 'yes' and Foggy said 'No!'; and, then Foggy asked him another question, and I whispered 'no' and Sam said 'no' and Foggy said 'yes!'; and, then Dr. Devine asked Sam a final question and I said 'yes' and Sam answered 'yes' and Foggy screamed 'No! sit down Mr. Williams'. Sam slid in his seat and turned and looked at me and for the first time the grin had left his face."

"Was he your friend after that?"

"Oh, yes. My point is that you should take care from whom you take your instructions because what is yes for someone else may be no for you and vice versa. What I'm trying to say is that many times your instincts are better than quick answers. I or someone else might, for example, help you with your game. All information is useful; however, eventually you'll return to the swing with which you were born. The beneficial thing about instruction and information is that like Joe Monk, you've got to know how and when to use it and you

22

must be able to absorb it all and to reduce it to its simplest so that on the course one thought or one recollection is all that is required to cause the lock mechanism to unlatch and all the pieces of the puzzle to come together thus freeing your natural swing. Too much information will only rescramble the puzzle."

"Oh."

CHAPTER FOUR

OLD WAKE FOREST

Spring, Nineteen Forty Six

This was the summer of Curtis Smead's high school graduation. He had won every tournament in Ohio and was now on the eighteen green at Flatbute Country Club, north of San Antonio, playing in the National Prep Amateur. On the eighteenth he was facing a left breaking down hill five footer to stay in the championship match. Buddy Purship had conceded a two footer on seventeen for Curtis to close to one down. Purship had made his birdie on eighteen, and Curtis had to make it.

He was slender, with a lock of brown hair hanging down over his forehead as his neck bowed rock solid over the ball, his knees knotted in that Smeadisk stance which later would be the key to his winning three Masters. He tapped the ball high on the putter blade, and as the ball neared the hole, the young golfer raised his head and extended his right foot in anticipation of a birdie well made - but the ball had made up its mind that the young man would not notch this victory; that his golf and immortality would be founded on lessons from defeats such as this.

"Curtis . . . one incredible match. I have never played against anyone who could rise from the grave as you always do."

"Thanks Bud. Congratulations, but I want you to know one thing: I didn't miss that putt, the ball did. You deserve to win, I've never seen you hit it so long."

"Curtis, by the way, where are you going to college next year."

"Well, West Virginia and Baylor have offered scholarships as have several other schools. It gets very cold in West Virginia, and Baylor is so far away..."

"Have you considered Wake Forest?"

"Well, no. Where is Wake Forest?"

"It's a small school in the Carolinas. It's near the sandhills region and is, as best I can figure, the closest major school to us where golf can be played all winter. Why don't you look into it?"

The bus had rattled all night down Highway 1 from Columbus. It was September. The campus, nestled in the forest of Wake and begun in eighteen thirty four, was

25

comprised of venerable red bricked ivy covered Georgian and federal buildings, sufficient to sustain a student body of approximately one thousand young men. It's uniqueness was its magnolias, the finest, largest and best preserved collection on any site in America, primarily as a result of the special topography enjoyed by this region of northern Carolina. This college village was not then known for golf, but more for the exploits of its over achieving football program and its legendary graveled voiced coach, Peahead Walker, and for its unrelenting quest for academic excellence and freedom of thought. Highway 1 was its lifeline as were the north-south tracks which intersected the village leaving the small college town on one side and the rolling sprawling azalea filled campus on the other. Wake Forest was then a Baptist owned school, founded on the principles of religious freedom, separation of church and state and the value of a liberal arts education and was destined to become, after its endowment by the Reynolds Tobacco fortune and its move to Winston-Salem years later, not only among the preeminent national academic universities but also, thanks in no small part to the athlete from Columbus, collegiate golf's perennial powerhouse.

It was onto this campus, after an all night ride down Highway 1, that the future king of golf arrived. He exited the old Greyhound with a suitcase in each hand and a golf bag over his shoulder, no strain for this muscular son of a golf pro from the North. Even then his blacksmith arms and thick hands foretold his slashing powerful style. The cock of the head and glint in his eyes were unmistakably Smead. Then, however, as he exited the bus, alone in this small southern village, how could he know what the future would hold.

"Hey!" announced two co-eds in unison to the young athlete who had never heard the salutation "hey" and who had not the least idea what it meant. He put down his bags still grasping his clubs to protect them against or from these strange

26

beings.

"Hi, can you tell me. . . do you know. . . how do I get to Gore Gym?"

"Walk three blocks down Faculty Drive toward the old well, then over the hill past Bostwich Dorm and turn left at the law school - then straight past three white houses, one of which is President Poteat's. If you get there you have gone too far so turn around and go back to Dr. Stroupe's house and whistle. After you whistle stand on your toes, look to your left, sing the Wake Forest fight song, and you'll be there."

Bewildered and tired Curtis squinted and grinned slightly, "Could I simply whistle the fight song?"

"No!"

"Look, I'm very tired, confused and away from home, and I sure would appreciate it if you would walk with me."

From that day Curtis Smead's love affair with Wake Forest was established. It was then and is now a campus where people always spoke, where friendliness was a tradition and where the David versus Goliath attitude in athletics was required for survival. It was here that he would learn how to win against the odds, for if there is a benefit to attending the smallest Division One A university in the country, a small private school competing against and competing well against the Marylands, Michigans and Clemsons of the world, it was the spirit and closeness that would propel this champion to become the athlete of the decade and the Babe Ruth of golf.

Well, Curtis made it to Gore Gym. He walked through the gymnasium that would echo during his days as a student with battles against neighbors N.C. State, Duke and North Carolina, down the stairs and into a small smoke filled room where two men sat: Coach Peahead Walker of football and Jim Weaver, then golf coach and later to become the first Commissioner of the Atlantic Coast Conference. There these three men met. "What's your name boy?" bellowed Coach

Walker.

  "My name is Curtis Smead."

  "What'd you play boy?" queried Coach Weaver.

  "I play golf."

  "Now, let me interrupt this story right here. Just for historical background, my grandfather, Elvis Olive, didn't know this information about Curtis Smead. Many years ago your grandmother and I actually were asked to have dinner with the great Smead and his wife Mary at the home of a mutual friend. My friend had a driving range at his home, and we hit golf balls there with this legend and enjoyed a meal together. Afterwards, we were sitting out on the porch as the sun went down, Curtis knew of my love of golf and of our mutual alma mater and volunteered this information about his first experiences at Wake Forest. I want to mention that here so that you might better appreciate and understand what follows. One more word about that dinner. What a friendly and compelling individual this champion was and is. No doubt his friendliness and the success which followed in no small part were derived from excellent parents, an excellent disposition, and a school which perpetuated these tendencies."

  Golf courses back in those days weren't what they are today and certainly at Wake Forest with its nine hole course and sand greens, there was much to be desired. By the way, Buddy Purship had enrolled at Wake Forest that fall as well. Coach Weaver had set out to build the program, and these two of the country's finest served as the initiators leading to the matriculation of others: Billy Joe Patton, who accomplished the greatest performance ever by an amateur at Augusta National, leading Ben Hogan by two shots going into number fifteen on the final round, to be followed by the team lead by Haas, Watkins and Bynum in nineteen seventy four, considered by most as the greatest collegiate golf team of all times and then followed by the many other outstanding all-Americans and professionals. Curtis' influence at Wake Forest was so great that in one year at Augusta fully one-fifth of the Masters field which made the cut were Wake Forest graduates. And it all started on that September day in Gore Gym.

Well, Curtis and Buddy got tired of those sand greens and were hired to convert the greens to grass for a charge of five dollars per green. That first spring after the grass grew Buddy and Curtis played every day, rain or shine, even through sleet.

"Curtis, lighten up. Your swing has become overly rigid; you look tense. I was reading an article by Bobby Jones in the Atlanta Constitution. Bobby says that we should hold the club like holding a baby bird. . ."

"Buddy, let me tell you something, when I have a plus two handicap, then we'll talk about me relaxing; but, until then - grip it like a baby bird? ridiculous: follow through like Walter Hagan? - never. Buddy, the key to understanding this game is understanding who and what we are both physically and emotionally and then unlocking and releasing our natural talent for golf.

"I've been studying a bit of philosophy lately: about fire, water, air, earth, fear, truth, success, superiority. Buddy, you have to go all out! The key to the grip is establishing the grip and never changing throughout the swing, and the key to the swing is the full release and that means no fear - that means commitment. If you and I are ever going to get where we want to get in this game, it will be because we have the mental strength, to commit through the ball for that one-fourth of a second when most people blink or shy away or start lifting their head - that critical point just before and just after contact where cowards or champions are born. I was out here the other day playing by myself, you remember Tuesday afternoon when it was so windy. And, Buddy, some things started to click. We spend all this time squaring up to the ball with matching lines made by our feet and our knees and our hips and our shoulders, and we establish the flight of the ball and our grip, and we determine our swing keys; we make a perfect back swing; and, then because of lack of concentration and commitment and mental toughness, we shy away from the swing and come out of it a millisecond early thus negating every good thing we tried to do, everything good thing preparatory to the swing. Buddy it all begins with the grip. It all begins with a strong firm grip, even a tight grip - not tight arms, but a tight grip. That signals to your brain purpose and commitment and resolve. You're telling your brain that you're not going to chicken out right at the end. That very day I made up my mind that if I never hit another good golf shot that I would go all out, swing from my toes and hit every club with maximum force and even fury; and, if that doesn't do it, it just won't get done.

"This morning good ole Dr. Reid looked me right in the eye after his philosophy class, and I know he was talking to me when he said 'Gentlemen, go all out, don't hold back in life or in anything else: if you learn anything from me at this school, learn these two things: don't fear success or failure, and polish your shoes every day.'

"Yeah, he really said that, 'polish your shoes every day.' Neither one of us will even get to the US Open unless we conquer this fear thing - and polish our shoes every day!"

"Curtis, some of the boys . . . they know you're the best, but have you thought that - well . . . that your follow-through

30

might be holding you back?"

"Bud, I'm always looking to improve . . . but think with me -my primary swing thought is the rock solid grip - firm, tight and in both hands, not in the fingers, in the hands; then the full backswing coiled tighter than my grip; and, then - the finish. Why all the preparation without results? So, the finale is the unbridled release. So how to achieve it? By hitting against something, and I create that something by bending my left elbow up as my follow-through nears completion - it serves as a break or a backstop to my release, like hitting against a rubber tire; and, I can release without fear of turning my hands over the top and snap hooking or cutting across or slicing. The finish is always the same with a twirl at the top - the final release of power."

"Uh huh, but . . . Curtis, it'll never get you to the great tournaments!"

"Dr. Reid's lecture and Curtis' own swing theories must have done Curtis some good. He went on to the win the individual NCAA Championship while at Wake Forest and the US Amateur Championship. Were his shoes polished every day? probably. What does polishing shoes every day have to do with playing golf. Good habits, pride, cleaning up your act, good image, a sense of order."

"Curtis, who is . . . who is that . . . fellow up ahead - there?"

"I don't know. But would you look at that swing. He's

31

playing by himself, and I don't think I've ever seen him out there. Come to think of it, the other day one of the fellows at Shorty's said that there was a fellow from over near Apex, thought he might be a black fellow, you know there are not many places where they can play down south, who got permission from Coach Weaver to play over here from time to time. They said he never plays with anybody, not that he sneaks out here but that he's a bit of a loner."

"Would you look at that swing. I . . . I . . . I've never seen - wow, it almost went in the hole, sucked back to three feet below the hole. And did you hear the sound when he hit the ball. I've never heard a sound like that. Let's play on. Let's see if we can catch him."

CHAPTER FIVE

DONALD ROSS

Summer, Nineteen Forty Six

The great architect returned to Pinehurst to build his home on the number two hole of the Number 2 course. His favorite time was late afternoon and his favorite walk was by the universally acclaimed green on the his home hole, later to be Tom Watson's favorite, of all holes anywhere, then on to the short dogleg par four to the right and then that mammoth par five, number four, downhill then uphill, a slight dogleg left into the future white columned World Hall of Fame; and, finally "the hole," famed number five, that awesome par four that flows slightly left across the rolling hills as natural and serene and as rhythmic as a set of waves on the ocean with an approach to the left onto a postage stamp green mostly requiring a three iron softly landed. But the great master was not satisfied, and the more he walked the more he pondered and queried within his own great mind as to how he could improve number four and number five. One afternoon he made a decision: he would bring together his men, including Benny Monk, to re-carve and re-shape and improve those two great holes together with several others. Mr. Benny was only too delighted to respond; and, within a fortnight he and Joe took up residence over the shop in the back of The Holly Inn. Joe was now fifteen and nearly had reached full physical maturity. His golf of late had been limited to playing in the low grounds and brief excursions to selected courses within the area primarily by means of connections that Mr. Ross had formed with those who came in and around Pinehurst in the late thirties. Joe was excited about the prospects of spending time at golf's mecca. He could still recall his limited times with Mr. Ross and could recollect the perpetual smell of tobacco which pervaded his presence.

That first Monday morning back in Pinehurst Mr. Benny met with the architect and several others, and Joe accompanied him.

"Me lads, me lads, the great men o Monk! I have missed ye, oh, how I have missed ye . . . Why who is this large lad? This is not young Joseph?"

"Yes, sir."

"Mr. Donald, this is young Joe. Do you mind if he stays for a while and even helps: he's got good touch with the mules, and I promise I'll stay right with him."

"Why o carse, me man, why o carse. It'll do me and ye goodt to see if the mules can train him as well as they trained ye - ah ha. Benny, I have walked and walked and walked over numbers far and five; and, I knew that ye would agree, we must reshape, we must . . . we must improve. Our masterpiece must be caressed. We don't want the ole girl to lose har bite, now do we?"

"No, sir, Mr. Donald. After driving our mules through Mr. Elvis' tobacco rows - now there's not much creativity in that . . . I can hardly wait to carve and whittle on "Miss Two.""

After the team reviewed the architectural sketches prepared by Mr. Ross, they all went out and walked the holes and set about with their "whittling." There stood the old great Scott, hands held above his head directing the mule teams not unlike Serge Kousseuitzky at Symphony Hall, cajoling the Boston Symphony, orchestrating the rhythm and the rhyme of the great course. Mr. Ross had spent hours listening to that great orchestra while he was in Watertown; and, he wouldn't admit it, but it was obvious what he was doing. He was directing his own orchestra as sure as if he were before the Boston Pops.

Work proceeded well. There came an evening when the rains had come and the crew had departed and young Joe was left to clean the shop, to curry the mules and to re-hay the stalls. Mr. Ross liked the animals, their strength and their smell, because - they were his brush, they were his motors, they were his engines - for he never used a tractor, ever - on any course. Some have theorized that part of his devilment was to leave sharp hoof prints throughout the course creating small divots to twist the blade of the unexpecting duffer.

"Joe, me lad, would ye come ere, please. Ye dad tells me that ye luv the game o gulf, do ye?"

"Yes, sir, I love to play."

"Then show me ye swing, lad. Har's me favorite clube. I do not show many o man this clube. It was givin me by old Laurie Auchterlonie, from St. Andrews, who taught me all I know and all I shall know about the game o gulf. It has been me walking kaen far these many yars. And as ye can plainly see, I have hit many o objects along the way and from time to time as I walked me carses."

"Thank you, Mr. Ross, but, am I supposed to hit a golf ball in this area?"

"Oh, me boy, do no ye worry. I've been har so long - you're with me - it's okay. Better yet, let's ye and me walk back down the carse over obout number ten whar we'll have plenty o privacy. Let me fill me coat pockets with sum balls. Thar, ye carry old Laurie's five, and we'll have us a marry time."

As they walked along the great man started talking. He told Joe about his childhood in Scotland at Dornoch; about his first lesson at the foot of old Tom McClarin; about the British Open; about Bally Bunion; Royal George and St. Ann's; St. Andrews, the old course; Royal Dornorch; Carnoustie and the great courses of the Rota, the courses of the British Open; about the wind and the sea and the burm and the chill and the rain and the challenge of Scottish golf; about the hard pan lies and the one hundred foot putts from the fairway and the gorse so thick that if one steps in it his foot is lost forever; about Bobby Jones coming across the great sea and winning the hearts of the Scots and those of the British Isles; about the story of those first Dutch sailors who left their ships off St. Andrews to walk across the dunes to the village hitting rocks with sticks amongst the sheep and the sand dunes where they hovered against the wind; and, about how the game began. It became apparent that the old architect, one time himself a player of championship quality, knew more than architecture, that he knew of golf across the seas learned from the masters who had no steel shafts, balata balls and perfect conditions, who stepped up to every hole and every shot and absorbed the situation and then regurgitated a perfectly formed shot, consistent with the conditions and in rhythm with their souls.

36

By the time they had arrived at number ten Joe Monk was limp with excitement. He knew of this man, and he knew that he was walking with greatness, and he knew that he was hearing things that no man had heard - but what he did not know was that he would hear more from this greatest of golf architects who may have been the greatest of golf thinkers and that now even this unique intellect was exploding with excitement with having young Joe there. But why? Joe could not know, and Joe would never know that Mr. Ross had known his mother; that his mother, who Joe never knew, was beautiful and gentle and sweet and athletic - that his mother was like a second daughter to Mr. Ross back when her father was on his construction crew - that he had overseen this seeming tragedy of pregnancy and with his dear wife, now departed, had counseled and nurtured Joe's mother in easing the burden with the decision that, at that time, she had to make. Mr. Ross never had a son, and he never had a grandson with whom to counsel and to whom to pass on the essence and spirit of life and of the game, both synonymous. Joe Monk could never know the joy and excitement in the heart of Donald Ross: a great man who with every step was realizing what was happening and was giving himself to the moment and the days to come that he would spend with Joe Monk down on the back holes of "Miss Two."

The secrets in the heart and mind of this man, reflections of centuries of play from across the pond, gathered from night after night of discussion with the masters. Now, and this was the time - to pass it on - to pass on secrets of the game that no one in America knew and that no one in Europe remembered, save one or two in Scotland whose bodies were too feeble or whose spirits were incapable of performing or articulating respectively the essence of the game.

As they arrived back to number ten, the boy and the icon already had become a unit and the lesson was joined.

"Joe, me lad, warm up ye muscles nicely, and then let me see ye swing at it."

"Yes, sir."

The young prodigy swung old Laurie's five iron back and forth, back and forth, back and forth, each swing a pendulum perfectly timed, the back swing a replica of the follow-through and the follow-through the second half of the first half without variance and without fail, and the great man could scarcely believe what he was seeing - even with a practice swing - the equal distribution of weight, the stationery and polar position of the right knee and right hip, the iliac crest, never moving back from the target but always supporting the absolute maximum extension to the nine o'clock position of the back swing, of the square position at the top with left forearm and the back of the left hand being flush as a newly plastered wall - old Laurie's five iron, at the top, being aimed - a laser - parallel to the target, with the divergence of the angle of turn of the hips and shoulders being more than Mr. Ross had ever seen - thus establishing a torque of the torso of unparalleled tightness and springiness. Old Donald could not wait to see the results of this storage of power and finesse: he dropped the ball, and without hesitation the young prodigy and old Laurie's five iron virtually exploded into the back of the white orb with that Crack! that announced vicious club head speed applied slightly from the inside, low and through and out to the three o'clock position and up high with both elbows pointed to the target, and with left leg straight and stiff to a follow-through that was held and could be held in perpetuity because of the ultimate balance of the initiator of the swing. The ball rose as if stunned, a bit low at first and then as if one of Mr. Benny's mules had kicked it with full force it shot out and up to a trajectory which ellipsed that of any the old master had ever seen - so high and with such dead straightness that the old man staggered backwards: then precisely one hundred ninety yards away the results of the prodigious effort landed the white object as a feather with one bounce to the right before it lay stone still, awaiting its tap-in, there at the tenth green of the second course. The old man gathered himself together with all his emotions and pride and realized that this was not the time to gasp or to praise - this was the time to challenge.

"Ah, that's fine. Me lad, indeed, me thinks ye have some talent" as the old man cleared his throat.

"Thank you, sir, but, Mr. Ross, when I play, I. . . get doubtful, and four shots will be as you saw while the fifth might fail me. Could you help me?"

"Why. . . why, yes. . . it shall be me joy!"

So there they stood the master and his pupil, without question the greatest raw golf talent the world has ever known or probably shall ever see again with the world's greatest architect and thinker of golf, past, present and, in all likelihood, future.

"Me boy, before we talk abut the swing, we first must talk abut the farse - because without the farse the swing is useless. Have ye studied ye chemistry - well, even though ye have, ye'll not have studied this. Ye see back in Scotland thar is a great university, and I used to read a buke by one o the professars. He was run ut o the university because of his fantastic theories, which I predict will be proven true; but, I read his buk, and I tried to apply his theories o the game o gulf. There are farses in the universe, thar is gravity that holds us to this gulf carse and brings ye ball back to the site intended. Thar is magnetism or more specifically electromagnetism and then thar is a strong farse and the weak farse which keep the protons within the atom and which maintain the electrons in thar intended orbit. Well enough o that. What I'm attempting to impart to ye is something I discovered. All o this electromagnetism theory is really about the electricity that runs our bodies, that carses through our minds and coordinates our

39

systems. We all know that electricity is conducted by sum things better than arthers. Far example, by water better than wud and by wire better than glass. Accordingly, ye might find that on moist humid days ye function better because ye internal electricity is conducted through ye system with the greatest ease and dispatch. Therefore, ye shall be a better golfer if ye do two things: fill ye body with fluids before ye play and put in ye bag some woolen cloth and rubbit at least every other hole and build up within ye the static electricity which will be conducted by ye greater mass of water which will enhance all the farses of nature not the least of which is the strong and the weak farses - and me boy, ye golf rhythm and ye life rhythms will have been maximized. Well, it's gettin dark, and I've been a talking a way too much, so we must start back up the carse or ye papa will worry. Can ye meet me tomorrow for our next session?"

"Oh, yes, sir."

As they two walked back crossing the fairways and through the clean pine groves the old man provided to the younger the preliminaries of the days to come.

"Joe, I can plainly see that ye grip is parfect - just parfect, and I can plainly see that ye mechanics are parfect - just parfect."

"Well, sir, what is happening to my swing when I fail?"

"Joe, ye lack just one thing - knowledge. Ye ar a natural swinger who for his brief life has relied apun instinct and feel and nothing else. Ye papa tells me ye can make a crow fly a different path and can provide a family with all the rabbit stew they could desire because o ye aim. That tells me that ye can intend a target and visualize with amazin accuracy; however, the game o gulf is not abut scaring crows and rabbits - ah, thar is much more to it than that - because ye must play on a carse designed by someone else, against another human bein, undar sum degree o pressure, seeking not just one shot but a calumniation of shots leading to a scare, hopefully ye lower scare. The sum total of these elements can sap from ye your natural flow and aggressiveness and can and have replaced it with just the slightest anxiety. Therefore, only knowledge o ye swing, only ye own ability to coach yeself, to correct yeself and ye swing on the carse will make ye the champion that ye can be. Well, Joseph we are just about hum. Now, I bid ye goodtnight, and do no think o gulf . . . ha!"

The next day Joe practically danced and sang his way through his work. "Joe, what's making you so happy."

"Papa, Mr. Ross is going to help me."

"I know."

At precisely six o'clock the two met again and started their walk back down to number ten on number 2.

"Joe, thar ar nine great lessons to this game, and I can tell ye aready know sum o them. Ye grip is firmness, is tightness, is correct. Ye ar a gulf carse creator like meself, and I can tell ye understand the rhythm and the demands that a carse requires, that ye know that ye must not fight the carse and the wind and the grass but that ye must absorb the scene and respond to it - ye aready know those lessons. And I can tell that ye know and apply a furious unrelenting fully releasing swing and that ye have no far and that ye'll never ever hold back from a violent swing with every clube, every time no matter the pressure. I shall teach ye the other lessons - but...but...that last lesson...I think...I'll try to impart it to ye, but many times a teacher must allow the student to discover it himself or the spell is broken. That is, the teacher might tell the student, but the student will never understand or if the student understands he will never remember. Now as we walk along let me remind ye o what I said last evening, and let me add to it. Not only must ye know ye game better than any other human alive, but also ye must become a philosopher, introspective, contemplative, always aware and always in control o ye mind, ye emotions and ye game; for it is in the control of these three factors that ye

41

obtain and sustain the ability to swing reactively, that is, without control; therefore, it's a matter of total mental and emotional control and knowledge which yields a totally physical reactiveness and involuntary control which yields an uncontrolled perfect reactive swing - the setup o mind and body is but half - the reactive release, the oter half. This is why great golfers luv great carses; each are reflections o the designers summonsing from us ar abilities to control ar minds yet freeing arselves to swing with the terrain and with the elements; and, as we discussed last evening, if ye can discover the designer's own thoughts, purposes and philosophies far every hole on every carse ye play and match ye rhythm and ye philosophy of play -- then every shot will be pure and every target struck. Well, har we ar again."

"Sir, may I ask you something?"

"Please."

"When I get to that fifth shot and my swing lets me down or when I let my swing down, I don't feel...I don't sense...I don't believe that there is any power, and I don't sense and believe and feel that I can get the club head to the ball - it's like the club head wants to hit behind the ball. I try to move my weight forward, and I lose my rhythm - then my club head comes over the top, and I cut it just a bit. Can you help me?"

"Joe, do no er forget what I'm abut to tell ye. Joe, it's ye head and ye hip. Farst, let me tell ye abut ye head. I do no car if ye head gues up and I do no car if ye head gues down and I do no even car if ye head goes back; but Joe, now har me, me lad, ye head must nevar proceed beyond the bul until after the bul is struck and ye ar pulled by ye own reactive motion to the left! If we had a movie camera with film fast enuf to stop every champion's swing, ye would see one thing every time and I mean every time - the swing o the champion would be demonstrated by a head behind the original position o the bul at rest until well past contact. It's okay if ye feel that ye even

42

push ye left cheek back to the right as ye hit the bul to the left. Ye see golf is a game o opposites. The amateur would think that by moving to the left with the head and the body the bul would go farther to the left and to its target; but, ah, to the contrary - by staying back to the right with the body and particularly with the head, until well after impact, the bul is compelled to go at greater speed. Now, the hip: that is the right hip - first, both hips must turn very little on the back swing in restriction and opposition to the major turn o the shoulders thus creating torque and the spring-like loading action o the upper body firmly founded upon strong legs and stationary hips. But, a problem all too common and very little discussed is the right hip moving to the right during ye back swing - a dastardly deed which contorts the body back and away from the ball, interrupts the torque build-up of the upper body and creates a lateral slide to the right and then back to the left during the down swing, causing a lunge into the ball resulting in a left leg that collapses to the left instead of staying as a stationary post and position against which the swing is swung. If ye right hip remains stationary ye become well founded to turn against it and then in combination with ye head which stays relatively stationary and always behind the bul the golfer becomes physically, and within the laws of physics, capable of repetitive action. Me lad, I shall assure ye that if ye will abide by me precepts abut the head and the hip, seventy-five percent o ye problem will be cured. Now what is happening har is a negative reactive process. When ye head and ye hip do not behave, the third factor that shows its ugly head is a restricted back swing, and ye know what that means - power outage. Thus, when ye see the golfer not only lunging with his hips sliding left but then lunging with his arms seeking power; and, me lad, when that happens, you might as well be shoveling chicken manure behind The Holly Inn; because it will bring ye must greater satisfaction then lunging at the gulf bul. Remember, thar will

43

be no power without reasonably stationary hips held against a fully turning upper torso storing power against a stationary right hip flowing by a head always behind the bul and a firm and stationary left leg as ye swing low and through and then high to a finish perfectly balanced. Now thar, whether ye know it or not ye have just been given lessons far, five and sex!"

"Thank you."

The young golfer hit ball after ball as the old artist sat on his umbrella with arms folded, pipe in mouth, smoke drifting skyward, from time to time closing his eyes enthralled by the sound of young Joe's efforts.

"Joe, tonight will ye join me at The Magnolia Inn. Some o the boys ar in tun, and we'll going to sit arund the table beside the big far in the great waiting room o the old inn."

"Mr. Ross, who'll be there?"

"Ah, there'll be a young fellow named Bobby Locke, whose been doing quite well in the Isles, and o carse you'll recognize the name Sarazen. But then thar is another man by the name o MacNicholos, an old friend o mine from Watertown, Mass, coach of the high school team thar, who just happens to be in the village . . ."

"Well . . . Mr. Ross, do you think that . . . I mean, what will they say if you bring me?"

"Joe, ye reputation will have preceded ye. Let's walk back up to the shed. Ye'll need to get cleaned up and meet me at seven tharty sharp at the back o the kitchen o the old inn."

"Yes, sir."

Joe arrived fifteen minutes early, and waited anxiously in the backyard of the inn, which also served as a chicken yard - only fresh eggs for the patrons of the venerable old inn. The Magnolia Inn is of white clapboard, its edifice built in the early years of the village and has housed all the greats who have played in the North and South. To proceed within the doors of the Inn, and for that matter within the doors of any of the four

44

inns of Pinehurst, is to walk through a time warp back to a period when the pampered guests arrived not on Highway 1, but by train only into Pinehurst station, there to rest their weary minds and bodies with golfing and horseback riding and hunting of quail and croquet, tennis and great food and bridge and above all, except for golf, the enthralling and mind stimulating conversation of geopolitical concerns and socio-economic issues and even metaphysics and religion and law.

"Hello Joe. Come on in me boy."

Joe stepped haltingly as he looked up into the doorway of the Inn. For the first time he remembered his clothes, for he now had two pairs of pants and three shirts, but still one pair of shoes. He had done what he could - they were always clean - but no degree of washing could erase the soft dusty look of wear. However, he had grown to be a strikingly handsome lad, with a profile now more akin to Victor Mature than anyone else while retaining that Benafonte carriage and always with an athlete's swagger. The young golfer moved with such grace that he made no sound as he entered the back of the venerable inn, accompanied his mentor and sat with Locke and Sarazen and Ross and this man MacNicholos. It was apparent to those present, those great and to be great, that Donald Ross was proud and excited and that the young man who strode so cautiously yet confidently into their mist possessed presence and charisma; he exuded athletic grace and power; and, as he extended his hand to each the grip was soft and firm, warm and the motion rhythmic, yes, even the shake conveyed a message to those there that this lad was an extension of God's creation as every golfer must be connected and a part of it all. These men had just finished supper and now were savoring dessert and coffee so black and aromatic that when mixed with the sweet smell of the Carolina pine logs burning one wanted to sit and close his eyes and absorb the very essence of the scene, the fire cracking as each turpentine pocket within the pine exploded, the room yellow with fire's light, the four Scots, flush faced from hearth heat and spirits.

"Joe, I've told these men about ye. Thar sits before ye Mr. Locke, the greatest putter I've evar seen and Mr. Sarazen, the greatest striker of the fairway wood I've evar seen and now ye, the greatest striker o the iron I've ever seen . . . yes, Joe, ye."

"Well, Mr. Ross, thank you, and, well, thank you. But I really..."

"Young man, Mr. Ross, has asked Mr. Sarazen and I and Coach MacNicholos to speak to you about the game. Since I have had some modicum of success as a putter I shall address that subject however briefly and then Mr. Sarazen shall complete our lecture and then we shall have a proposition for your consideration."

"Yes, sir."

"Try to miss every putt, that's my secret. There was a time when I putted well, and then it was gone. In the middle of the night after trying everything - every grip - every stance - every swing key, I determined that I had nothing to lose; why not try to hit the ball just close enough to miss it every time. Pardon my immodesty; however, the next day in the final round of the British Open at Carnoustie, of twenty three putts I tried to miss, unfortunately I could miss only two; therefore, I made twenty one.

"Now, no one knows this about me, and I don't think anyone knows this about the game. If you will free yourself to fail and to miss, you will free yourself to be a champion and putting will become fun. I understand that you hit the ball so close to the hole that you don't own a putter . . . but even you will have to make putts, and by trying to roll the ball very closely to the hole, I promise, that you will not be able to keep it out of the hole."

"Thank you, Mr. Lock. I promise, tomorrow I shall putt

a thousand putts back down on the number ten green, and I shall attempt to miss each and every one of them."

"Ha, ha! That's just what I wanted to hear."

The architect added several logs to the fire and the flames struck higher and higher and more coffee was poured, together with whatever else was in the cups of the champions, and they settled back with rosy cheeks to hear the words of the great Sarazen, the man who had struck the shot heard around the world - that rifle-like four wood against a Wilson ball at the fifteenth hole at Augusta into the setting sun, the ball rising over a fairway fluorescent green and into the hole for an eagle two.

"Joe, there is just one thing that I can tell you. There are many golf clubs in the bag and many shots required. But for all of us there is a best club and a best swing amongst them. But for some reason we tend to attempt to utilize different swings for different clubs notwithstanding that we think we're using a basic standard swing for all clubs. Again, ninety-nine point nine percent of all golfers, even though they think they're using the same basic swing; in fact, they are not, and they are manipulating the club by trying to swing differently with a two iron than with a nine iron. Let me tell you more specifically, for me my best swing is with my sandwedge. Now, I'm not going to tell you how I developed it, and why I developed that club and my development of the sandwedge has nothing to do with the point I'm trying to make. It just so happens that my best club and swing was and is a sandwedge. In the past the swing of my two iron and of my driver absolutely were different from that of my sandwedge. Not only was I more upright, not only did I take a more deliberate, lengthier swing with the longer clubs, not only was I not as free with those long clubs - I lacked finesse and purpose and freedom with my swing. With the swing of my sandwedge I would open my stance; I would slightly open the club face; I would then push

47

the club head very low and very straight and very lengthily away from the ball with finesse and purpose and with my left shoulder and would then swing with abandon and outward and would slide the club face under the ball with much right hand feel and control, the ball reacting to the club face like water off a tin roof bouncing each time upward from the club face and consistently so. Moreover, I could open and close the club face and make the ball go literally straight up and could make the ball dance left or right or dash forward or spin back based on the finesse imparted by my rhythmic and natural swing and the finesse of my right hand. Of a sudden it occurred to me, would this swing work with a two iron? We golfers are a strange bunch. You have your experimenters, and you have those who stick with the same swing for their entire lives. There is much to be argued in favor and against both of these propositions; however, as an experimenter even I have found it difficult to attempt radical swings. I would go out on the practice tee and just try anything and everything: all the grips, all the setups, all the ball positions, from short back swing to long back swing - from ball to the left to ball to the right - from ball closest to my feet to the ball being away from my feet and for some reason, though I have and would try all of these swings I objected to and fought a natural tendency to swing a two iron or a driver or a five iron as I swung my sandwedge! After a particularly frustrating second round in the U.S. Open at Marion, I talked to myself and said 'Eugenio, your game is going south, you have nothing to lose - let's give it a try.' So I did! First with my nine, then with my eight, then with my six, then with my four, then with my two and then with my driver. I set up like I was going to hit my sandwedge and with a slightly opened club face, forced the club back low to the ground with my left shoulder and hand, and turned to a full back swing and a full risk cock and then exploded under the ball with full righthand force propelling the ball to a trajectory that I'd never felt

48

before!! So, obviously I'm describing my sandwedge swing: set up with the feet and the shoulders aimed to the left of the green or the fairway; open the face slightly; push the club face straight to slightly outside and very low, that is the key, the clubhead must be pushed back very low with the left hand; then after a big shoulder turn and pronounced wrist cock, delay the hit and drive the clubhead low and through the ball with the right hand releasing toward the left side of the target area; and, even feel that you're keeping the club face open to the sky as the face glides under the ball and throws the ball up; and, the final element: release but don't release, that is, it's like bumping into the ball - your hands turn over and your forearms pronate - yet not ever quite fully, thus achieving a long high fade and a ball that floats downward and lands like a mosquito on a green pond. That swing and that form resulted the next spring in that four wood into the hole at number fifteen at the National. So, my fine young man, don't use anything but your best swing for every club."

"Joe, are ye counting: seven and eight - you've just heard . . . do you understand?"

"Why, yes, sir, I do understand and thank you Mr. Sarazen and thank you Mr. Locke."

"Now, Joe, it's time to tell ye why Coach MacNicholos is har. All three o these gentlemen war dun by number ten last evening during ar little lesson. I hope ye do no mind me asking em thar to witness covertly ye game?"

"Certainly, why, of course, not - I'm honored..."

"Now, Joe, the only thing a gulfer wants more than far himself to be a champion is far a champion no to be wasted, far championship talent to be realized. In the heart and soul o every gulfer is a teacher o himself and o others. As in life with goodt things, it is incumbent upon us gulfers to pass along every scintilla o knowledge that we gain so that future generations can be enriched and can enjoy not only an athletic pastime but also a means to explore the soul and spirit o man. Joe, we think that ye can be a good golfer; no, I might as well say it - we think that ye can be a great golfer; and, a good teacher must tell his student honestly what he thinks o his ability. I far that if no one tells ye the truth about ye game that ye will never know and attempt to realize ye great talent, and unless ye believe ye're great, ye can and never will be great! Joe, we want ye to play in the Narth and Suth, if not this yar, within the next several yars. But, thar is just one problem, and it's a problem that we hate because of those who have created that problem. I might as well just say it, Joe. Because ye ar black or part black, ye're no allowed to play in the Narth and Suth, ar far that matter in any arther sanctioned tarnament. Sum day that's going to change, but that day has no yet cum. Joe, I hope ye will forgive me, but I've told these gentlemen of ye parents: that ye ar black and that ye ar white and that ye ar a fine young man - potentially a great young golfer. To qualify far the Narth and Suth ye must win a state tarnament at least, and ye must be white. Well, the latter is easy because I say yar're white enuf, but the former is no so easy . . . Joe . . . ye must go Narth; and play; and win; and then . . . return to the Suth as a . . ."

"But Mr. Ross, I can't leave Papa, and we can't afford..."

"Joe, we're getting ready to address those two problems: Mr. Benny is all far this; I've talked with 'em, and he supparts ye and us in this endeavor. Secondly, muney is no object. Just please do no ask any questions; muney is no object. Now about Coach MacNicholos . . . as I told ye earlier, he was my goodt friend in Watertown. Watertown is a lovely community just west o Boston and right next to Cambridge and Sudsbury and Harvard University, along the Charles River. It was me home before coming har. It just so happens that the Watertown High Skul gulf team plays at me old carse, a great

50

carse, a majestically beautiful carse that overlooks Watertown, the James River and the City o Boston and which was designed by one of gulf's greatest architects, Alister MacKenzie. Joe, we want ye to go to Watertown and go to skul and larn from Coach MacNicholos and play with the Watertown team and play far and win the Massachusetts State Amateur Championship and then return to North Carolina to the North and South and to yar future."

"Young man, I've spoken with a family in Watatown, the Brown family. They have three boys, a hockey playa, a football playa and a promising young golfa. I've spoken with Eddie, Scott and Kevin, and they want you to come be a part of their family. Kevin particularly is excited about having you thar. I promise you, you'll like our town and our people. There probably is prejudice everywhere but maybe less at this time in history in our area because it is a melting pot for immigrants. The suth with catch up with us, but it's just going to take time: they've no had the benefit of the melting pot experience; certainly their people are just as caring, yet their experience has been different - but they shall larn - one day prejudice will die."

Those five unlikely comrades sat by the fire for four more hours, sipping their coffee and whatever and thrilling each other, but more particularly Joe, with stories of golf tournaments around the world, of matches within matches, of the nuances of the game, of equipment, of the future of golf and of the future of golf's greatest natural talent, who sat there with them attempting not to demonstrate his own doubts and insecurities.

"By the way Joe," assured the coach, "it's easy to get to Watatown. All you have to do is go north on Highway 1 for eight hundred miles, and you'll run right into it!"

It was misting lightly as Joe walked home down the quiet dark avenue known as Dogwood Lane, the avenue thick with moist air, dense hollies and southern foliage, each step making less noise than the other as he turned to slide through a pine grove thickly carpeted with thousands of brown long leaves of pines now beginning the process of slow decay which eventually would lead to new life in that old forest - and his thoughts were of the farm, of tobacco, of his grandma; and, he could hear the life sounds in this forest, emanating no doubt from cousins of the tiny creatures which had eased him into sleep in his loft over the low grounds.

Did he want to leave? Why should he have to move north to qualify for a great national tournament? He'd never felt prejudice or known prejudice . . . that he could remember. No one in Olive Chapel or at Pinehurst called him boy: he didn't expect any more than he had so why should he want more than he could take? Wouldn't it be better to hit rocks in the low grounds than to be lonely way far away? Things had gotten away from this grandson of the poor tenant farmer and son of someone from Waltham.

"Joe Monk, why do these famous men take interest in you?" he mumbled only to the enclosing darkness. What is it about this game that would cause men such as these to reach down here to help Mr. Benny's son to be what he wasn't sure he wanted to be in the first place. Four months ago he was driving mules over dirt and now he has a chance to go to places and meet people of whom no black boy in Olive Chapel ever dreamed, and why should he want to meet... he had heard that in Boston there were Germans and Italians and Polish and Armenians and even Greeks, right off the boat - if he didn't know prejudice in the South, how did he know that he would not meet it in the North - but in different languages and among strange and indifferent peoples. For the first time he felt a fear just below the bottom of his stomach that resounded periodically to a point in the center of his chest, right in the center of his chest where his two lungs met, and he couldn't make it go away and right then and there he wanted to go back and say no.

Then something come to him that Miss Pearl had told him as he watched her ring a chicken's neck, and then pluck dinner, "Joe Monk, everything that ever happens to you will be your own fault. You can never blame any other soul for what happens to you. If a man spits in your face, he can't hurt you unless you say it hurts; and, if you don't make no more of yourself than that rotten potato in the patch, it wasn't cause you didn't have a mama or because you worked the tobacco fields with your bare feet, it will because you decided that you wanted to be a rotten potato. Joe Monk, you live in the greatest country in the world! You see how Mr. Elvis and Mr. Benny plant seed, and you see how those seeds grow and flourish and how we top and sucker the tobacco and prime it and hand it and loop it and cure it, sort it and take it to market, and then the next year we do it all over again. It's hard work - but it feeds us. But Joe Monk, if Mr. Benny hadn't planted that seed, we wouldn't have any tobacco or corn or tomatoes or peas. So tonight, when you say your prayers, plant your seeds - but, when the plant grows - don't be afraid of the harvest."

And then it hit him, what Mr. Ross had said, all that preparation, smelling the course, checking the line, setting up to the ball, the full turn and the stored power, the concentrated mind effort and conviction that will lead to a proper result . . . and . . . then just before impact, a millisecond of doubt and fear . . . "No!" Joe shouted to whatever was out there; and, he knew that it was time for the harvest.

CHAPTER SIX

OAKLEY AND WATERTOWN

Winter, Nineteen Forty Six

He had never known such cold; yes, he had seen snow, but never the wind, off the ocean. He just couldn't get warm, but he didn't care as he surveyed a scene like none he'd ever experienced: of Oakley, a course unlike those in the Carolinas which were low and rolling and protected on all sides by trees - this one was over and around and on a small mountain rising from the river James, with Boston lying to the east, and to the south, Watertown, and beyond, the James as it snaked westward through Waltham and Weston and Waylon and to

Marlborough. He was quick, and he was smart, and he had studied the land of our revolution. He knew not only of Revere, and Faneuil Hall and the Old Meeting House, but also of Longfellow and Thoreau. He knew he would never go to college, yet three miles east down Mount Auburn Street from the square at Watertown was Harvard Yard and Cambridge and the beauty of the red brick trimmed in white, which was Harvard.

"Come on man, let me show you numba two!" called Kevin Brown, son of Ed and Dorothy, and great-great grandson of a real American Indian, a Nipmuc. Joe knew no indians. Were people prejudiced against indians?

"Ya see, Joe, numba two comes out of that shoot down theya, does a slight dogleg left, and then to the green ova theya."

"Where, Kevin? There is nothing but snow. I don't see a green."

"Use your imagination man!"

"At least man was better than boy," Joe thought to himself.

"And then number three ova theya, the tee to the right of numba two green. Numba three is a pa three; now you've got to keep it to the left up on the hill and let it bounce onto the green - otherwise you're dead. . . man. Now come on over hea - hea's numba foa, a pa five down the hill back toward Belmont Street and then on the left hea is numba five, a pretty good pa foa."

"Where?"

"Why, you're practically standing on the numba five green. Can't you see it?"

Yes, now he could see it - there, under him and the snow, the green and, yes, there - the bunker; that had to be a bunker under that two-foot snow drift. Joe knew greens - but Donald Ross greens.

55

"Kevin, who designed this course?"

"Some MacKenzie fellow . . . Alista, Alista MacKenzie. Good architect, I think - at least my dad - yes, my dad said he was a great architect, from Scotland!"

"Do the edges of his greens always form a crest and a crown?" Joe asked getting more excited as the conversation progressed.

"No, silly! Why would any idiot design a golf course like that?" And Joe knew that a golf course whose greens were not like an upside down dinner plates were duck soup in his capable hands.

"Now, away theya, just beyond the numba foa green - that's the tee to numba ten which runs along Belmont Street. Well, you wanted to play golf - so let's go play golf."

"Golf. Today?"

"Yes, we have an indoa golf range. My dad said it was the first in the country - I'll show you the rest of the course tomorrow," as two cross-country skiers slid by the two young athletes with a swoosh!

In Watertown, every house was huge - something about Catholics, families, birth control and all that. And the high school on Columbia and School Streets, right there in the middle of town, not a city but a real town, even this close to Boston - neighbors and kids and children everywhere, with big St. Patrick's right in the middle of it all. These were Catholic people, not Baptist; but, he couldn't tell the difference, and he wondered if the Pope and his Reverend Jeremiah Overcash from Olive Chapel Baptist would be friends . . . of course.

From Boston along the Commons and by Back Bay over the Salt and Pepper Longfellow bridge and by MIT to the right, Boston University to the left and then Harvard on both sides and then a rise along the river at Watertown from which one sees that small mountain on the sides of which large houses sit warmly protecting these hearty people, one crest of that hill

56

being Watertown, and on the other side Belmont, arch rivals; and, beyond Arlington, Winchester, Woburn, Lexington, Bedford, Concord; and, except for a city limit sign here and there, one never could distinguish where one town ends and another begins; but, what he liked best was that these were towns not cities; and in them - working people.

There, in the somewhat dimly lit Oakley practice facility, homecourse of Watertown High, stood the pro O'Hara and the Coach MacNicholos, and the team, all hitting balls thirty yards into a net.

"Joe, come hea!"

"Yes, sir, coach."

"Gatha round, boys, I want ya to meet Joe. Joe these are ya teammates. Ya already know Kevin, and this is Victor Canino, and theya, Armand Keutchakien, Brian Lancaster, and Johnnie Georgeoplis, Aldo Vidritch and Amelio Cappola and Kasar Keutchakien, and . . . yes, he's on the team too, he's just a freshman, Roberto Leone. Gentlemen, this is Joe Monk from Carolinar - he's a playa. Joe, do ya fellows eat barbeque in Carolinar?"

"Yes, sir."

"O.K., after practice, I'm taking ya all out to Redbones. We need to fatten Joe up."

And over to Summerville they went, and it was right there that Joe Monk knew he could survive in Boston. They piled his plate with red beans and rice and slaw and on top, beef ribs and pork ribs and barbecued chicken and around the edges, cornbread absorbing the juices of the other and making Joe wonder if southern fried chicken was all that great. The boys and Coach MacNicholos sat around the table, and Joe learned of Italian Catholic families, and they learned of tobacco and cucumbers and catfish - but nothing of crows and rabbits and rocks and sticks, for soon enough they would learn that this prodigy was their savior.

Until April there was little opportunity for golf so Joe studied, got a job at Redbones washing dishes and lived with the Browns on Cuba Street just around the corner from St. Pats. In his spare time he returned to Summerville and the shops along Harvard Yard where he did as he was told, he walked and looked and listened and absorbed the scenery just as if he were playing a round of golf along those streets and through the campus and down by the river. He loved the undergraduate library. He read the books of the great golf masters. He had been challenged by Mr. Ross to discover the ninth lesson himself, and he remembered that Mr. Ross said that it would not profit him for anyone to tell him the lesson; that unless he deduced it from thousands of balls hit and thousands of hours played and after frustrating rounds, that it would never mean anything . . . that it would be like one of those vapors that Mr. Ross constantly discussed. But how could he find this ninth lesson among all this golf knowledge? Mr. Ross had given him purposely several hints: "the key is on the right . . . the key is like a 'k'." What did he mean, and how could Joe possibly unlock the truth?

Spring finally arrived and within two weeks Joe had established a Massachusetts handicap at plus two and had attracted the attention of the Watertown and Belmont sports writers although not those in the greater Boston area. With Joe at number one and Kevin at number two and Victor at number three and Amelio at number four, these four Americans with blood from Italy, Romania, Africa and the American Indians cursing through their veins, they turned in scores and set records that will never be equalled in Massachusetts high school golf.

When Joe Monk's handicap reached plus three, the Boston press took notice. He was interviewed and a nice story was written on the third page of the sports section, which Coach MacNicholos quickly dispatched to Mr. Ross, who laid it on the table of Winfield Eleredge, Chairman of the North and South Committee. Coach MacNicholos had chosen Kevin and Joe as team representatives to qualify for the Massachusetts State Amateur to be played in July. The war was over and the young soldiers who survived had had time to return and to fine-tune their games with the result that many older and mature golfers would be participating - more than in prior years.

Joe and Kevin both qualified for the match play portion of the tournament facing Massachusetts' sixteen best amateur golfers. During the practice round, Kevin, now with a minus one handicap, noticing that Joe seemed a little down and stopped him. "Joe, what's wrong?"

"Well . . . I'm a little worried. In yesterday's match I hit two shots in a row, high and to the right. I didn't recover, and I made double bogey. Kevin, it took all I could do to qualify for match play. I wish I had Mr. Ross here."

"Well, if ya don't mind me saying, I noticed that ya right elbow appeas to be a bit high; that is, when I stand behind ya, ya shouldas aren't open, but ya right elbow is a long ways from ya right hip. If I remember correctly what Coach MacNicholos told me last yea, that means you've got to come ova the top just slightly in the down swing."

"The right elbow, uh? To high...okay. I think I've got it."

The door opened slowly, its glass front embossed "Black Literature." Like all the other shops around the Yard at Harvard, it was small and clapboarded and one-half story up, above the street, and one-half story down, below the street - a lower level for living or whatever.

"Come on in, shy boy!" implored and mocked did she

from behind books stacked highly on the floor for marking before display.

"I . . . I was just"

"You sound different - yes, the south - are you a southern boy?"

"Why, no, I'm from the north - - - of Carolina; ever heard of it!"

"Shy boy, I've never been south of the James River, east of Backbay, north of Bedford or west of Weston, now how do you expect me to get to Carolina; and, why would I ever want to go to such a forsaken land?"

"How old are you - twelve, eleven - I'll give you the benefit of the doubt - thirteen?" And Joe dropped his head and waited for the explosion.

"Fifteen!"

"Fifteen!?" He pretended astonishment.

Her black eyes now reflecting the white light from the street which lent some pink and some tan to otherwise porcelain skin, and the shine of curls, wavy, serpentine and midnight dark and flowing below her shoulders; she obviously was fifteen, at least, and a rose now budding, as Joe seemed not to notice.

"I'll bet you don't have a girlfriend in Carolina - you're too shy!"

"And why would I care - whether - a thirteen year old cared whether or not I was shy . . ?"

"And you're not a student either - so don't pretend to be one!"

"Little girl, where I come from, little girls say 'yes sir' and 'no sir' and . . ."

"Yes, sir, Mr. non-student shy person from the north of wherever - I'll bet you heard I was in here - a provocative experienced woman!"

"Well, actually I was looking for a book about black

golfers and . . ."

"And what would you know about golf, or what would you want to know about golf, and why would you want to know it . . ?"

Joe had never had a girlfriend - and never wanted or needed a girlfriend, and he hadn't had time for one anyway. Never had a girl so white talked with him that way or flirted . . . was she flirting - he didn't know and didn't think he cared; but, he came back two days later - she said she might know of a book about black golfers in the big library, as Harvard: she would help him order one from the card catalog in the library - but he didn't have any money any way, so what good would it do to order from a catalog? When he finally was introduced to the card catalog, he knew he'd been taken, and among the millions of volumes tucked in that venerable old building across from the chapel with the tall white spire with the cross of gold above it, where future presidents read, there was not one to be found about one black golfer, no not one.

Later they walked and talked, and he hoped she was at least sixteen, but he didn't care as he was lead around, now like a bull on a chain, the northern flowers seeming to open in rapid succession - he'd never noticed flowers; why did he notice them now, and why this insouciant urge to pick them - but he did; and, then, one night he kissed her . . . . . . and from his stomach to his brain orange sparks like those that rise when pine slabs are thrown on embers to heat the barns back home, and his ears and the back of his neck collected those embers, those sparks and he grew heated with the warmth like the well-fired crop heating in midday in those oven barns of the deep south; but, he was in the north and as his hand touched her neck and her hair, her sweet smell made him feel light . . . what was happening, was he losing control - who was this yankee girl . . . and she kissed him again, then he withdrew and again that flowery scent - certainly she was seventeen, he hoped and he stopped! And her head fell to the side with a sigh . . .

The Massachusetts Amateur was no challenge. Joe Monk won the final match six and five and really wasn't trying. Kevin made it to the quarters and then to the semis and was grateful that he didn't have to play Joe.

As Massachusetts State Amateur Champion Joe started getting invitations to play in tournaments around the state and around the area and around New England. Mr. Ross sent him a letter of congratulations and acknowledged that Coach MacNicholos had mailed to him the article in the Boston Globe together with Joe's picture finishing high and on balance of the twelfth hole of The Country Club. And, of all things, Mr. Ross included an application for the North and South and a note from Mr. Elleredge inviting this young "Massachusettsian" to play in April, with the nation's greatest players, in Pinehurst. Now, Mr. Ross made no mention to Mr. Eldredge of Joe Monk's past, of his lineage. Mr. Eldredge was new on the scene, having been transferred in by the Director at Pinehurst from the Atlanta Country Club, this man, a member of Augusta and soon to be a member of Pine Valley. The Board at Pinehurst had appointed him as tournament director of the North and South. Mr. Ross was only moderately concerned; he did not know much of this man's past, but certainly he was an accomplished industrialist, and now, the czar of this greatest of southern tournaments.

All the arrangements were made. Dorothy, Ed and the boys bade Joe a tearful goodbye as he boarded the bus to travel back down Highway 1 from his new home to his real home to do what no one thought ever would be possible, play in the

North and South, with a chance to win, and with them, Victor, Amelio, Roberta, Kasar, Coach MacNicholos and, of course, oh yes, Savannah Book, his beautiful Eurasian friend. But Joe was not sad, except for Savannah, because he felt that now he had two homes and that he could return to either. After all, this trip was to play in a tournament, a tournament which if he won, would open the doors of wealth and riches and international fame and invitations to the U.S. Open, the PGA and even the British Open. Yes, it was time to harvest, to heed Miss Pearl's words.

All the way south Joe's mind recalled his destination, many scenes of which he had almost forgotten and the people and the food and the life on the farm and even the sanctity of Number 2. Joe had forgotten what it was like to live with space, not that he didn't have space up North, but an openness of territory and lack of people density which creates a slow restfulness and pace of living whose only negative aspect is recurrent loneliness; to a place without Greeks and Italians, Polish or Armenians; to a place where people either were African or White and of those, either English or German; but, even they knew not which. Joe had learned that there is a pecking order in every community and state; that one race questions the worth of another; that people in medium size cities think little of those in smaller cities while not realizing that those in larger cities think the same of them, and so on and so forth. He'd been amazed and hurt that some in Boston did not know whether it snowed in Carolina, and then he realized that many in Carolina did not realize how much it snowed in Boston, and his heart ached for one reason - that having met these people in Massachusetts he wanted to meet more in other places, for he loved people. Golf was his ticket to the world. He was free, he was talented, he had been challenged and he was ready to gather. Now he couldn't imagine any one thing that could stop that, whether he realized the ninth lesson or whether he didn't. He was talented enough to play among the best and to win his share.

As the bus rolled along west of the Hudson in the darkness the world was black and gold, all black except for the millions of lights of Manhattan and surrounding boroughs, a sight that he'd never beheld, his face reflected in the small greyhound window, his big brown eyes absorbing every photon of light from that majestic scene; and, for some reason that scene and those circumstances placing his innermost spirit transcendently both above and within it all and like every true golfer at a moment like that, he related it all to his swing, to the flow and the rhythm, the timing and commitment, and he could see his swing and its every element. He was getting closer to fulfilling Mr. Ross' admonition that he must be his own best teacher; that unless a golfer could envision his own swing and every movement, he was subject to the uncertainties and peculiarities of each circumstance on the course - so Joe concentrated on his swing, and in slow motion he could see each blade of grass as the sole of his club brushed by them on the backswing, and he could see the wrinkle in his trousers, each of which signaled a move well made under the garment and such things as the position of his belt buckle and the manner that his shoe laces lay upon his feet as they founded and transferred power from the earth to the ball - he concentrated, still seeking the ninth lesson with just a twinge of worry if he could never find it: because even Joe Monk knew that he was fallible - that the game has always been greater than the greatest player and that no, not one had ever fully conquered it.

As Joe rode south on 1 toward 2 he felt full and satisfied because he had consumed the Massachusetts countryside as only a golfer can consume it. He knew that when others travel and see sights of great beauty that fill the spirit with excitement, that all but golfers must leave that scene unsatisfied: it is only the golfers who have discovered a means

64

of topographical consumption that not even the artist can know. One round of golf over strange and beautiful countryside requires the player-farmer to dig, to toss, to smell, to wade, to brush back and by playing and traversing God's earth and by the connecting of dots formed by each shot from the first to the eighteenth, the player, as suredly as a giant whale sweeping everything before it and sifting that which is tasty through its baleen, so the golfer sweeps over and consumes the beauty and the majesty of the earth as no one else can. Joe Monk had tasted Massachusetts, and now he wanted to taste the world.

"Papa, are we there yet?"

"We're getting close. You see that building up ahead in the center of the highway - that's the Chatham County Courthouse, and we'll circle around that courthouse as it sits in the intersection of sixty four and five o one and then head on to Olive Chapel. This is where Miss Pearl taught school as did her oldest daughter, your grandmother and where my father came to see her from Lexington on weekends; and, there is the school where she taught on the right. Now think of it, your great-grandmother and your great-great-grandmother both taught here and one went east and the other west, always connected by this highway, each a teacher from Meredith - it was all so natural, one following the other, and that's what made it so strange for Joe Monk leaving his home, for of all places Boston. That, was important - for him to see other sights and places and courses, and grasses and to feel the air and the smell of the food and the houses along the courses. The biggest mistake a young golfer can make is to play all his rounds on one course: if it's too short he learns not how to hit long; if the greens are slow or fast he's at a loss, and, most importantly the hills and the flat places. There are so many variables: the green where your target can be above you or below you; the ball, above your feet or below your feet; or, you can have an uphill lie or a downhill lie or more wickedly than that a combination of the several factors. Now remember this, for a slight hill always add a club, for a moderate hill another and an extreme hill another - then you must factor in the cool air which calls for greater length and a breeze whether light, moderate or strong in your face, the results, literally a nine iron shot might recompute to a one iron shot. It can happen, although not commonly. We're going to play many courses, are you ready?"

"You bet."

CHAPTER SEVEN

THE NORTH AND SOUTH AMATEUR

Spring, Nineteen Forty Eight

Joe and Mr. Ross talked late into the April night as he described for his benefactor every shot of every northern round. Mr. Ross awaited each word and reveled in the excitement fully detectible in Joe's tone - but the main subject was never mentioned, the final key. Mr. Ross particularly was interested in Joe's friends and new family and new girlfriend and even his new church, the old historic stone Baptist church at Harvard Yard just in the back of the majestic Inn at Harvard Square.

"Joe, tell me about that church, who were the people

who went there; were they all white?"

"Mr. Ross, this was a white church, yet they had a special ministry for new black arrivals of many counties, and I felt most at home and a special kinship there, as I did at the great Catholic church there in Watertown. Mr. Ross, I was reared a black man; yet, there I was accepted as a white man, I guess, because of my complexion and all the rest - they had no reason to question whether I came from Mr. Benny or Mr. Elvis. It was so wonderful being white, not that I don't love being black. I sat where I wanted, ate where I wanted and walked where I wanted and was not questioned - not one time. It was different when I got off the bus in Richmond and needed to use the bathroom and was hungry and wanted to buy a sandwich. I began to realize that I had lived without prejudice on a southern tobacco farm and without prejudice in the far North but had never lived in an environment where real prejudice existed, whether in the North or the South. Mr. Ross that is something that I just could not take. If I'm not accepted, I will never ever impose myself on anyone or any group of people. I must admit that I am still a bit shaken from that Richmond experience. But, I'm glad to be home."

"Well Joe, me lad, ye ar all signed up. The tarnament starts next week with the greatest field in history. That new tarnament in Augusta is becoming quite popular, and I har that ul o the international playars who play thar the week before will be traveling narth tu Pinehurst. Committed to play ar Frank Stranahan frum America, Remers Dugan frum Scotland and Singjan Smithe Willinghast frum Welles and even Charleston's Johnstone Ashley Merrelle, as well as all o the top college players. Joe, ar ye ready?"

"Mr. Ross, it's just a matter of a stick hitting a rock aimed at a rabbit's tail!"

The world's first outdoor practice tee was filled with the world's best golfers that Monday morning on April twelfth. The practice tee lies contiguous with and to the left of the eighteenth hole of Number 2 and contiguous with and to the right of the eighteenth hole of number four: behind it and to its left sits the renowned Pinehurst Country Club, and away and behind each - the number one holes of the other courses, closed for parking and traffic and attendant services, all in honor of her majesty Number 2.

There is no sound like the sound of the accomplished golfer striking the ball with forged steel and persimmon; and, the sounds on that practice tee were the sounds of great golfers, in rapid succession, striking balls - but only one man was there who struck the ball with a sound like none other - the unmistakable Crack! There was not one golfer or spectator who had failed to notice the never before seen high hands of his back swing and the contorted twist of his follow through leaving both shoulder blades forming a line fully perpendicular to the direction of the ball at the target. The first two days were medal play with the top sixteen qualifiers moving to match play.

As Joe teed off at number one the chimes of the old Presbyterian Church to his left, only a nine iron away, rang the hour ten times as his ball rocketed down the slight decline of the number one hole, those church bells slowly playing a hymn of grace. Joe now was splendidly attired, thanks to Mr. Ross, with oxford brown and whites, light gray woolen double pleated fully cuffed trousers and the white golf shirt crisp and well ironed, just like Hogan's. The prodigy strode into the sunshine and the light breeze from the northeast as if sent from his family and friends in Watertown reminding him to breath deeply of the pine scented southern air.

Joe went out in thirty-three strokes without a sweat over

one of the world's great courses, five birdies and one double bogey, just a lapse but nothing to worry about.

On the back side he cruised, not wanting to break his spell and finished his round at sixty nine, well in advance of any score required for qualification purposes.

That night Joe rode with Mr. Benny back up Highway 1 to Olive Chapel to eat with his grandmother, to say hello to Mr. Elvis and Miss Pearl and to remember his past. But Joe was going for a greater reason, he hadn't forgotten that doublebogey, and more importantly he didn't know what had happened. He tried to put it out of his mind; and, like a seed that can grow to harvest, so can a thought grow to a doubt and a doubt to a fear...

They stopped for a brief visit in the Miss Pearl's dining room by the fire under the single light from its cord from the ceiling as Joe told Mr. Benny, Mr. Elvis and Miss Pearl something of his Boston adventure; and, they were proud as if he were their own son; and, they chuckled at the excitement of this eighteen year old who had become articulate and charming and even urbane.

And down the dirt road they rode, past the milk barn on the right up the rise and down to the crest of the low grounds where the road becomes a tractor path down to Joe's very own country club. The nights are still cool in April in Olive Chapel and the smell of wood smoke from Miss Ursula's kitchen stove and collard greens and ham frying and those - those biscuits swelling in the intense heat of that old iron stove made Joe wonder whether anything in God's world could be better than that; he knew that there wasn't. Well, the first thing Miss Ursula wanted to do was to make sure that she ridded Joe of any and all evil ideas which had attacked him from the North and from foreign peoples. She was proud and when grandmother's are proud they feed, and they stuff, and they want to know why you are not eating more: so Joe, ate and inhaled the sweet lemon nectured tea and topped it off with more until he felt right puffed and a bit bullfrogish.

After supper Joe and Mr. Benny walked down the tractor path to the low grounds and talked of many things for this was an emotional time for Joe, but he didn't fear emotions or what all this might do to his game, because all of this was part of his game, and he couldn't separate himself from it. Mr. Benny left him alone there in the darkness, and Joe removed his shoes and rolled up his trousers and walked through the cool tan sandy soil where he had plowed corn and tobacco and had primed and plucked and picked and fertilized and harrowed - back half way to the tree line into which he had to that day never entered, and he thought about his future and his lessons and one more piece of Miss Ursula's pie.

They rode back to Pinehurst that evening, back up the dirt road with one light on in Miss Pearl's kitchen as Mr. Elvis was eating his sweet potato and drinking his Pepsi Cola, the elixir of sleep for the son, grandson and great-grandson of tobacco farmers.

At New Hill they turned right on Number 1 and south toward Number 2 and Joe dozed and thought of his swing - and tried not to doubt.

Tuesday dawned cloudy and cool, the old course taking on a slight Scottish chill yet with barely a zephyr, the practice tee again resounding with the sounds of the accomplished at their game. As Joe finished practicing, his eye was caught by the slashing, vicious swing of a player over to the far side of the practice tee. He had never seen a swing like it or heard a sound so nearly akin to his own, this iron man's swing ending curiously interrupted as if his left arm were hitting a wall half way into his follow through, and then the club seemed to twirl at the top and then fall limply with both elbows out.

Joe's round that day was a round of fewer birdies but with three bogeys, all in a row ending on the eleventh hole - but significantly, he did not know why, so he forgot it and accepted his even par round leaving him among the top ten of the sixteen final qualifiers for the start of the real tournament.

To be champion Joe was required to win but four matches on Wednesday through Saturday. Dugan had made it, as had Wellinghast, Merrelle had not, but Stranahan had, as did fellows Krouse, Wall, Grimsley and two collegians of whom he knew nothing.

On Wednesday morning the practice tee was surrounded fully by fifteen hundred spectators with only the sixteen players remaining. Joe's warm up was uneventful, and as he shook hands with Willinghast he saw to his left Mr. Ross with his umbrella seat, his hat and his pipe and a twinkle in his eye. Inspired Joe birdied the first, second and third and was two up after two and was three up after nine; and, as he strode down number ten after a prodigious drive, he thought back to his conversations with Mr. Ross and the lessons he had learned. It was windy that day and both players were satisfied with par at the fifteenth, where the match was conceded to Joe at three and two. He learned that evening that his opponent in the quarter finals would be Dugan, Scotland's Remers Dugan, from St. Andrews.

In the kitchen of the Holly Inn there was a small room where Mr. Ross from time to time would dine alone. As a part owner and a legend in his own time, and near the end of his days, he needed to get away. It was there that he asked Joe and Mr. Benny to join him for supper. They discussed the day's round and the rounds of the other players. Now there were but eight left including Joe, Stranahan, Dugan, Wall and the two collegians, one of whom had defeated the great Grimsley, nine and eight!

"I did no watch any uther match today, but tomorrow, Joe, if ye'll forgive me, I think I'll check on sum o the uther boys, sort o scout 'em out for ye."

72

"I would very much appreciate that Mr. Ross, but I'm concerned about you walking all these holes at your age and..."

"Now Joe, Number 2 is me child, and she'll take care o me. By the way, Benny, when this tarnament is over, you and I need to go ut and harness old Bob and Tom and reshape the green side bunker at number far - we can do better. And Joe, this Remers Dugan, a grandson o the old tavern master when I was a student at Edinborough. Strong stock those Dugans; I kin guarantee ye this, he'll no let up a mit!"

On Thursday morning a crowd had gathered around the practice tee swelling to twenty-five hundred souls watching the eight that were left.

. . . click . . . click . . . Crack! . . . click . . . click . . . click . . . click . . . click . . . Crack!. . . . the sounds of the practice tee had lessened and were more distinct, and to the rehearsed ear of the master could be heard six clicks and two Cracks! six clicks and two Cracks! and the great Ross cocked his head for the origins of the sounds - he knew one, but not the other; and, there away by himself was that man with arms like a blacksmith and hands of a welder; and, even from that distance Ross could see a grip as firm as Joe's - tight, unrelenting, purposeful - as the man thrashed and beat at the ball with utter fury, each time hitting that wall of a follow through and each time cocking his head left and right as he stared at the ball grimacing, metaphysically forcing it to follow his intended path. Ross thought to himself "I'll follow that man today."

After three holes Dugan was in the lead and one up. Joe had hit one of the worst shots in his memory and for the first time in years conceded a hole, the second hole, Ross's home hole, without even putting. Well, nothing to do but move on. The great Scot amateur was short and thick with a swing so fast that even the cameras of today could not have recorded it. Never had Joe seen a ball dance on a green, and even a hard bermuda green, the way and in the manner of the ball of

73

Remers Dugan. If his ball hopped one time too many or too few, the stocky Scot would expound expletives under his breath with a snort and with multiple r's that made young Joe chuckle to himself. By the ninth hole the match was level and remained so to the fifteenth when Joe decided to turn it on, which he did. Mr. Ross came out and congratulated both golfers and invited Remers to dinner with Joe and Benny in the kitchen of the Holly Inn.

As they sat there that night savoring the salty bacon soup, Mr. Ross looked concerned.

"Joe, tomorrow you play Wall, and that leaves the collegians playing each other, a surprise to everyone except themselves."

"Ah, Mr. Ross, ye have nothin about which tu worry. Nobody can handle your man Joe, for he has been trained by a great Scot, one of me own; and, any man who can beat me is going to win this tarnament."

"Remers, me lad, I hope ye're right."

"Mr. Ross, I've been thinking. I know the final lesson is for me alone to discover, but would it hurt me to have another hint?"

"Well...Joe...let me think . . . okay, boot this is as far as I'll avar go; and, Remers, ye listen carefully tu."

"What is under shall be over, and what is inside shall be on top, for strength lies close to you."

"What is under shall be over, and what is inside shall be on top, for strength lies close to you?"

"That's rrright, and that's ul I'll avar say abut it. Joe, ye, must find it yeself."

"Yes, sir."

Word had filtered throughout the Carolinas and the South about those four who were left: the great amateur, Wall, who everyone knew soon would turn pro and who had been a favorite from the beginning, and now these three unknowns:

74

Joe and the two collegians. Then the committee was being asked to accommodate the press from New York, Philadelphia and Chicago. Wall the prohibitive favorite was faced only with an eighteen year old. There were now fully eight thousand people following these two groups as they meandered the seven thousand yards of Pinehurst Number 2.

"It will serve no purpose here my child to belabor this match. Joe Monk won it, but it wasn't easy. He suffered a double bogey on three to be followed by three birdies and then a triple bogey on nine followed by a birdie, a par and another double bogey. Clearly, he was like a fighter stunned, and the look in his eye showed he was searching, even begging; that doubt had clouded the flow of his swing, and if he didn't pull it together, even the great Joe Monk could not survive the championship.

"Well, Joe won it with a par on eighteen, the great Wall having lipped out a four-footer for par as he stood with his hands on his knees amazed that this youngster from Massachusetts, unheard of, could defeat him in such a dogged match.

"And that night Joe laid down his head and said his prayers and tried to chase from his mind the doubt and all the time he retraced his golf memory for something that might awaken his subconscious to that one last functional swing adjustment that most assuredly would win this tournament and propel him to a limitless future. He had slept but a few hours when he saw the sun break through the blinds of his room signaling that the day and the match were here."

Seven hours before, the phone had rung at Two Pinehurst Boulevard and was answered quickly by the old master in the bedroom of the white cottage immediately adjacent to the landing area of number three on Number 2.

"Yes, Ross, har?"

"Mr. Ross, I humbly beg your pardon, sir. This is Winfield Eldredge. A matter of some concern has been brought to my attention."

"Why, whadt in the name o the Royal and the Ancient coud bi uv susch urgency?"

"Mr. Ross, I'll come right to the point. I received a call, an anonymous call, this afternoon from someone who made the outrageous assertion that Joe Monk might not be of Massachusetts but might be of area lineage, if you get my drift."

"No, sire!"

"Well, Mr. Ross, this . . . ah . . . anonymous caller made the assertion that Mr. Monk might be a local or from these parts and that he might be descended . . . by that I mean, well, you know . . . that . . . well, Mr. Ross . . . I'm from Atlanta and, sir, I detest these kinds of things . . . but . . . well, this man . . . said . . . well he mentioned the Klan and . . ."

"Ah, now me boy, this Klan is nothing but outlandish rubbish, and me advice to ye is - let's ul get a good night's sleep preparatory to tomorrow's epic match."

"Yes, well, I thought maybe you could reassure me, and I can't imagine there being any problem . . ."

CHAPTER EIGHT

THE EPIC MATCH

April, Nineteen Fifty-Two

Since he couldn't sleep he got up. It being just daybreak and still cool, he slipped down the back steps from over the shed behind the Inn and in and amongst the magnolias and the hollies and the azaleas and the dogwoods he stepped lightly: the doves cooed softly down beyond sixteen as he crossed the fairway at one and silently strode to the green at sixteen, for his mind had been filled with those last three holes; and, notwithstanding hundreds of other prior visages, he sought one more look at the serpentine par five and the devilish par three and then the eighteenth uphill back to the club house as broad and expansive as a great runway but now green and misty with only the ambulant light reflected from low clouds in fog, all of which looked green and pinkish and somewhat gray: for he loved the look of it and had become addicted to this art work of grass and earth and sand and pine which later would be framed by speckles of white and pink, red and yellow and some dark green, the garment of the people who had come to frame and see and stand quietly and applaud; and, then - the roar, the echo akin only to exploding cannons in a valley, a roar that only can be heard from sound reflected of pine bark muted by long pine boughs - conveying messages as clear as the printed word that the man in front or to the rear had birdied or bogied or better or worse, every skilled golfer knowing the feeling when conveying or receiving those messages, and Joe knew that he wanted more - not just tomorrow but many tomorrows at Newport and Baltusrol, Carnoustie and Bally Bunion and Colonial and Hope Valley, then Oak Hill, Oakmount, Seminole, and Augusta: was it the golf or the people . . . it was the experience, the highs and the lows, each course a cathedral created by The Creator and slightly improved by man, if he didn't do too much, the sky over each ever changing from dawn to dusk, with more beauty than the stain glass at St. Peter's or the alabaster of St. Paul's.

Warm-ups were complete and the two younger golfers, one eighteen and one twenty, were brought together before those fifteen thousand plus who were in back of and down each side of number one on Number 2 as the President of the Board invited the two combatants to shake hands. The strong collegian with a warm smile, his muscular hand thrusting forward to Joe, "Hello, my name is Curtis Smead."

Joe did not know why those words would have this affect, but his knees slightly buckled at the sound of the name. This collegian from up the road at old Wake Forest College had attracted the attention of a good many national golf writers; yet, he must prove himself in the North and South and at the US Amateur later in the summer.

Both men, more natural as collegiate running backs than as golfing competitors, each broad shouldered with slender muscular torsos - it was those forearms - Smead's; but Joe's strength, hidden by woolen trousers - his thighs, full and thick; his feet large and agile; his foundation his strength.

There was not an ounce of animosity between the players who immediately realized a kinship. They knew the sound of the other's shots; and, they realized, at least in their innermost selves, that their arrival on the world golf scene signaled a major turn of golf's highway from light and slow and smooth to viciously tight, strong and explosive. It would be these facts that would excite the world of golf and propel the game one hundred fold to greater heights than Jones and Vardon ever could have imagined.

"Your attention please, ladies and gentlemen, now driving, from Columbus, Ohio and Wake Forest College, winner of two NCAA Championships . . . Curtis Smead."

The crowd hushed as the collegian set his overside driver, black and polished, its freshly wrapped leather grip sticky against his kid glove, as he wrapped his powerful hands engulfing all but the bottom inch of the grip: the sky now misty blue, the sun just clearing the pines over the right rough; and, Donald Ross watched toward the green, back up the lovely grade which formed in reverse to the tee a dog leg right, and the chimes of the old church rang the hour ten times as Smead forced the big driver low and wide, the ball rocketing from the gold tee sat on green bermuda ever skyward with a thunder sound, and as it rose to the right of the fairway bunker it drew, as Smead's shots always drew, and dove as if it had eyes toward the downhill slope and tumbled and then gently settled as if awaiting its next command.

"Your attention please, ladies and gentlemen, now driving, from...from Watertown, Massachusetts, winner of the Massachusetts State Amateur . . . Joe Monk."

Joe saw a bird two hundred and fifty yards out and fifty yards up and without a thought or a care aimed his spalding dot for the poor aviator's right wing tip - Crack! - the sound of the dot leaving the tee in the still cool Carolina air like the sound of the surf sizzling to the shore as it bore through the mist - the silence ended by a collective gasp - for well over half of those present had come just for this day and had heard but had not seen the prodigy. The bird dived but just barely as the ball never moved from its line, so high that it carried to the spot where his opponent's ball now attentively lay and jumped to the right with a bounce, there awaiting its master.

The two, still uncertain of the other, strode separately away and away from their caddies until a more natural time for small talk and efforts of respect that each yearned to convey.

As the old master watched, his heart pounded in sequence to the stride of his student, and as he strode closer his pride swelled within him, for this man, the son of Benny and Maggie.

The pin was front right, one pace from the crown sloping from the green and on a plateau, the size of Miss Pearl's dining table; but it was no matter, for Curtis' well struck nine with a twist and a grimace fell within a yard as did Joe's soft wedge - all square, birdie birdie - resulting in a buzz of excitement through the throng now larger than any yet seen in the Carolinas.

Number two of Number 2 extends directly onward away

from the club house in a straight line from number one, another par four. Curtis' brown forelock already in his face with black and white oxfords, black floppy but neatly pressed trousers with old gold shirt, his alma mater's colors for good luck; and, Joe, why change, he couldn't, the same oxfords brown and white, gray slacks and white shirt as on each day he wore because he had no other.

Curtis still with honors and Joe then followed with drives identical to their predecessors. Number two, four hundred thirty-eight yards, with pin back right required three irons of both with the results equally spectacular, short putts for birdies - was this a game, a clinic or a dream? How can such golf be played by any man before thirty thousand eyes of humans and countless more eyes of fellow creatures who must tire when their enchanted park is tread upon by the golfing masses. Both men had conceded the putt of the other, "that's good" in unison, and both said "thank you," and smiled and moved quickly to number three on number 2, as the thousands approved, all white, save one black, a man named Benny, who Ross had fitted with a uniform and a rake, serupticiously to walk and to pray.

The number three hole continued the extension of one and two from the club house, but was quite short and doglegged right with the required approach over sand and sage, the signature of all Pinehurst courses and particularly this.

Curtis' four wood skidded by the corner and landed two feet from the left far rough leaving him seventy yards in; Joe's two iron bisecting the fairway one hundred yards back.

As these two walked forward the silence was broken. "Joe I understand from Coach Weaver that you have played from time to time at Wake Forest. I think I saw you there one day - yes, now I know - it had to be you. I admired greatly what I saw."

"Why, yes . . . Coach Weaver was called by Mr. Ross

because . . . well I needed to experience other courses, and thank you for the compliment."

Already, over half of the crowd had proceeded to line long flowing incomprehensively beautiful number five while the competitors on three lofted first a wedge and then a sandwedge with shots that smothered the white flag helplessly flapping as if to tell the golfers that the course lay defenseless. No concessions here; simply a four footer and a five footer struck squarely to the back of the cup, and the match was all even with both men three under. Match play it was, but each knew that the other was three under and smoking.

Number four is from an elevated tee to a landing area twenty yards across slopping slightly right to left with sand and long grasses on either side, then the hole rolls gently upward to the left with the green set in a grove of towering majestic heart pines, a hole tailor made for Smead whose drive ellipsed all others that week and with familiar draw it hit and rolled to three twenty - still two twenty uphill to the flag. Joe noticed the narrowness of the driving area at that prodigious distance so he took dead aim at a tuft of naturally growing love grass two ninety up the draw and imagined a white cotton-tail - the ball rose high and higher, and out of the corner of his eye Joe noticed Curtis squinting to follow its flight. The great Deamon Deacon seemed to shake his head as he hitched his pants and trotted down the tee knowing that Joe's ball, as usual, would be slightly ahead.

Of all the holes at Pinehurst the walk down and then up the lovely gradient of Number 2's second best hole is an epic journey for any lover of the game; and, scarcely a word was said, even by the gallery, as they followed in the fairway and in the rough, their champions with a slight wind in their face. On approach Curtis' three wood bounded twenty feet above and to the right of the hole which was left middle, Joe's one iron stopping ten feet below, left.

As they walked stride for stride -

"Curtis, what's your favorite course?"

"Oh, that's easy - at Scioto where I grew up, where my dad is still the pro - and yours?"

"Oakley, in Watertown, Mass . . . you can see the river and the town with its church and school and large homes and then to the east the great city; it's not only the course - it's the vantage the course provides."

Curtis' putt broke severely left. He imagined that he was putting down the tin roof of Beacon Smead's storage shed at Scioto - these greens faster than either competitor ever had experienced, and five feet out all present knew that more feathers would fly - from wings of eagles. For the first time that day Joe felt slight pressure obscurely in his heck as he lined his ten footer, it obviously right to left with a two and a quarter inch break; and, he would try to miss it: the result, the talons of to a second eagle landed on that green, and all the old boys knew that the first four holes of the old course had just been played better than any two ever had; and, each player knew that the other stood five under after four.

The legendary gold tees, back fully, as the competitors stretched up to the fifth tee which oversaw golf's preeminent flowing dogleg left, devastatingly long, a par four, the signature hole, and the hole by which others are judged: number eight at Pebble Beach, sixteen at Oakmont, thirteen at Augusta, eighteen at the Country Club and two at Carnoustie, eleven at Royal George and St. Anne's and seventeen at St. Andrews - no - for no hole compares to it: this majestic par four built over three waves of sandhills each so perfectly drained and weathered by thousands of years of elements, a hole which had preceded him by millennia and which Ross knew better than to alter except for a tee, a green and the slight leveling and smoothing of God's ground topped with a sprinkle of seed and fertilizer; and, it sprang forth to overwhelm the mighty and to

83

inspire the slight as the crowd mumbled, discernibly restless, as if awaiting a skater's lutz - the players' blades on razor's edge, these gallant surely must topple soon for the golf gods are watching and would not and could not let stand effort past perfection else the game might ever fall from grace in the hearts of men and their Creator; and, the players knew it and sensed it, and the caddies were fidgety as each mindlessly handed his master his one wood, and with each practice swing it seemed that butterflies lifted from this shady scene of deep green garlanded with white lace of springtime dogwood blooms, the great hole lined with white sand and high grass and down the center a black-green carpet waved in the direction of the clubhouse and then back to the left of the green at number three; the green at five surrounded on all sides by dogwood with white and pink, each blossom having a golden eye and each peddle a brown scar which southern legend holds was symbolic of the cross. Would the younger ever gain honors in this match of legends to be? . . . the to-be great Smead held nothing back as he applied golf's first lesson and perfectly melted the flow of the shot with the flow of the land - up and to the right, up higher still into the blue sky and sun met ball, its reflection looked of gold; and, as the land dove left so likewise the ball, but only slightly as it drew then attacked the turf bounding to two ninety, left center and only a four iron away.

On the tee Joe recalled his right hip and carried his hands high and back over his head, reaching farther than he had reached before seemingly not caring if the trance were broken and understanding the destain felt by the spirits of the game - but he did not falter and the extra extension effected a towering blow, a high fade, uncommon for him as it flew two eighty five to extreme right center ending at three o five, a mere six iron from home. The two were not talking nor was the crowd and to the left through the pines could be seem the ever slight trail of the old man's pipe and his dark gray tweed and red plaid tie, his four squares ending at the top of equally grayed socks which extended to old scottish oxfords last worn on the day the old course was opened and now worn to revive all good fortune.

The ball was slightly above Curtis' feet - he was aiming to green right with the flag back left and with a hitch of his pants and his natural draw, the hole awaited him now tame to his attack; his shot was well struck ending precisely in mid-green, providing his longest birdie attempt of the day. Now Joe saw an opening! He remembered his right hip and his head and kept them precisely in position. As the clubhead ripped through the course bermuda wire he moved to his finish -- the sound was not right, not a crack but a bit less, and Joe's ball was hooking - not extremely but enough, as the fifteen thousand strained to follow its path, thinking surely that this great man had aimed at a rock to the left of the green, which would propel the orb directly to the hole - but not to be; and, the ball sank into the Carolina sand behind its grass, with the bunker between the ball and the hole, Joe Monk was human after all - no one need be told; and, with a grimace and sigh and then a shrug, he slumped, then moved forward, his lie surely a plug; yet, he felt relief as he tossed, the club to his man, and strode confidently toward, his ball in the sand, and old Donald had seen it, and he wasn't surprised - that his prodigy had wilted, to his Rossian enterprise - but Monk was mortal, for at the end of this hole, not one man was mistaken, Joe had been too bold. A bogey and a par on the scorecard they marked, and they marched on to six, like a walk in the park, and Ross sensed that Joe, was now thinking too much, as his student scratched and stood, and then slumped there to putt, on the number six tee, at one ninety a challenge, but the battle was joined - Joe had thought, now was gallium.

Joe knew what he had done so he decided right there to

stop thinking, that he should just be there. He knew the basics; he was now his own coach. He believed in his source - and there was no circumstance on any course, through which he could not reason and deduce in a season. Smead sensed blood; he was older, and now could look back and remember a time when at eighteen Stranahan had caused him to buckle - by thinking too much. Smead had reached the next level when a golfer can think but not think, when he's found a swing engaged by big muscles along with triceps tightly to chest - a connected swing which produces few birdies but guarantees pars under mind-squeezing pressure, and now he knew, that pars would do, and that his connected swing, could insure that pars were the thing, to beat this young talent who had succumbed to his charm - Smead still up; the one change he made, to stop that follow-through a might early, with left elbow high - no hook or slice possible, this king of sport had his prey coiled within him, and with each breath Joe took, Smead squeezed a bit tighter, both his grip and his stare signaled a predator superior, and Joe's shot was pretty, and that was about all, as its fall was unsuitable.

To absolutely no one's surprise Joe fell again - now two down at seven, but with everything to win. It must be his hands, their position too low, so he set them forward, before his blow, but that didn't work either, on this dogleg number seven, as the ball flew right, in the rough of golf heaven; while Smead laid up, his brown arms the anaconda, and they bulged and Joe gasped, his air from down under. Smead's shortness was deliberate as his shot flew first to its target with perfection and down to the earth: Joe Monk saw it all, and bent at his waist, then stood and stroked, quickly with haste, now not wanting to think, but thinking nevertheless, as high hands had failed him, and so did the rest - his head must be forward, not too far back, his backswing inside, now outside - then erect; and, around and up, to a position never before felt, Joe's swing was a wreck, and so was himself: old Donald could feel it, and was crying inside, for his boy was now feeling, the whip on his hide: three down then four and five for the side, number nine yielded no better, as he continued to slide: to the back side they strode, number ten a par five, nine holes to play, and then they'd decide. His life ran before him, the low grounds and home, Miss Pearl in her kitchen, now all alone; he stood on the tee, and watched Smead move with such grace, like he had nothing to prove, at this stunning place; poor Joe was a mess, his swing no better, a miracle was needed, he had to confess, but he best not digress, from intended objects in proven form, he again felt some confidence - akin to the norm; but, doubt had oretaken him, and driven him down, as he walked on the hole, where more bad shots would abound - and when it was over, number ten was a flop, his shots not a crackle, but a sound like a pop: six down after ten. Joe felt discouraged, and utterly incapable, of mending his courage . . .

"Joe . . . Joe . . ."

"Oh, ah . . . Mr. Ross, Mr. Ross I'm sorry, I . . ."

"Joe . . . I believe in ye Joe."

"Mr. Ross my game . . . where has it gone? I've been over the eight lessons, forward and backward and have tried to envision a swing; but, I can't. If I just had that ninth lesson . . . I might have a chance."

"Now Joe, I cannot do it, ye're ul on ye own, take it and use it and call it ye own, remember the K and the under will over, and the last will be farst . . . Joe I believe in ye, and I luv ye no matter what - it's only a game - it's only a carse . . . . . . but it's ye game . . . . and it's me carse . . ."

As the old man drifted back into the crowd the young golfer stood as if in a fog and every lesson and every stroke of his brief history spun through his mind in microseconds, and again he could see a part of his swing, the flow and the rhythm, such a simple thing: the fog became whiter and more clearly he

87

saw the young boy swinging sticks and like the thaw of springtime those frozen imagines melted and visualized that day - that day at Oakley with Kevin - - his right elbow - something about his right elbow, what did Kevin tell him? What did he say, and what was his message on that cold February day, in Watertown on the hill, at Oakley they walked, where MacKenzie and Tufts and Ross had stalked - so the key must be there, in that common place, and if that were not so, he was displaced, from his rightful position . . . no; stop - no more rhymes . . . only truth . . . what did Kevin say . . . th el . . . it was too high; and, as he rotated the backswing, flop and let it fly . . . no no no more rhymes . . . the right elbow was higher, than the left, causing his shoulders to spin early, and the clubhead to rest, at an angle now open, so clearly despised, giving rise to a ball, that did nothing but rise, to the right high and lofty, and weak did it fall, with results that were awful, and appalling to all . . . no more rhymes . . . wake up . . . think . . . . the key . . . the "K" . . . could it be . . . that which is low, "that which is low is really above" . . . the "K", the key, that which is low . . . "and ye shall find power within ye far sure" . . . . no more rhymes . . . power from within me, the K, the right elbow, inside - - - the right elbow inside - - - way inside and low and close . . . in an instant he awoke as from asleep, but for a moment . . . the crowd never noticed, and the Crack! awoke him, like a smack in the back, and he reasoned, and reckoned, and reacted to attack . . . to move forward and onward, from eleven on home, this young man had the last lesson, down deep in his bones, and it never would leave him - not ever - not ever, and to guarantee him his place, and his home forever, on the world's great golf courses, just leave him alone, and let him play golf . . . and let him play golf . . . and let his play golf.

"Joe . . Joe?"

As Curtis laid his hand, on Joe's shoulder, Joe awoke from his trance and strode over . . . to the teeing ground . . . as if . . . in slow . . . motion . . . not wanting . . . to bear the emotion, of the knowledge . . . of the truth . . . of the ninth lesson - - - if it were not so . . .

This, a par four, flowing from near the Pinehurst famed stables back toward the outward nine, this farthest reach from the famed old clubhouse, this a place that would mark Joe's future. It was easy now - survey the land, the wind, the pines, the grass, the sand, the flow, the rhythm of God's earth; and, the grip - firm and tight, but not the forearms, and the right hip stationery, and the hips restricted as his big shoulders turned the full extension, with hands high but not too high and his head slightly tilted, but never to move forward . . . never to move beyond the ball before contact . . . the practice swing felt good, but he forgot one thing - the K, the secret, the right elbow in and tight - as at contact. Joe couldn't bear a practice swing that way, he would try it preparatory to his full swing, and his commitment would be absolute. As he strode up to the ball and established his stance, Curtis knew in an instance . . . things were different, and so did Joe as his right elbow nearly touched his right hip so . . .
still -

"CRACK!" and Joe knew - Joe knew that HE HAD IT! that he had discovered within his own agonizing failure the holy grail of golf, that ninth lesson which combined with the eighth, the golfer's best swing with the golfer's best club mimicked with all other swings and clubs to produce with a tight elbow well in to the left at address a pattern and a form to guarantee repetitive swing and groove. It was now so clear to Joe, and it was so simple - to set up as in the exact position at impact only made sense - but nobody did it, and it looked a bit strange; that sandwedge swing which like Sarazen's was his best just didn't work with that low, protracted take-away forced by the left side until and unless the right elbow were nailed in position, at the beginning of the swing, and held there until impact - and the ball rose and fell as Joe knew it would, and as Smead knew it would from the sound of the contact; and, Donald smiled: he knew Joe had found it, "the keys in the K, and over is under, and the end is the out, for a swing like thunder," he mumbled to himself as he interposed the hints that had unlocked the secrets and connected the dots of an immortal swing, synapses of the mind now galvanized perpetually, rockhard and eternal. Now Joe would never fail to achieve his goals . . . even those of his mentor.

Curtis' approach was short and to the right. Now Joe struck the followup blow - for one swing does not a champion show - but the shot was perfection. What would the great Smead do now under such unrelenting pressure - he chipped in of course, then conceded Joe's putt - with a wink, and a slap, on Joe's butt.

Joe knew he was five down, with six to go, and Smead knew the same, but what would it take, for Joe for win this game . . . and then Joe won thirteen with a bird, and a second and a third, fourteen, then fifteen, those classic par fours; and, Curtis' face wore a frown, Joe now only two down.

Then sixteen, a par five, stretched like a green serpent, flat down on the ground, all curved and foreboding, its head the green's mound; and, as they walked it, they felt it, almost rise and fall, as if alive, only sleeping, now what would befall; it's back ever arching, a crown on both sides, to play it was treachery, now no one denies, and each knew what faced him, if minds focus failed, for in a brief moment, disaster beheld - - ah, the lure and the challenge of Ross' reptile - - the master's creation, they were compelled to abide, as first Smead, then Monk dug his spikes in its hide, the snake hissed and threatened, as again it denied, to these warm blooded mammals, on the old famed backside, no better than par - alas it decried - and - to Smead a bogey, now one up - again denied.

On to seventeen, and a birdie, by Smead, a par three, but

the great Monk scored an eagle, did he, as it dived in the hole, just under the tee, at the long eighteenth, where all would see, Joe Monk take over, then walk with such glee, to the final hole - all even was he, while all wondered together, whether Joe could keep going, in spite of the weather, for a dark cloud was gathering, from Candor to the west, and under it were walking, four men in black vests; intent on some mischief, mal-intended were they, but none in the throng, could hold them at bay; and, Joe drove forward, ore the bunker on the right, then Smead struck next, oh what a great flight; and as they walked, the men came closer to say, "Joe Monk you're the best, but it's just not your day;" and, as Joe approached, just like the other, the ball fell and jumped, and provided a cover, that hung o'er the cup, but did not go in, then Curtis struck his, before they would sin, those men in black vests; and Curtis' came to rest, on the fringe far away, from the ultimate, cup of the day, and just before these men had finished their play, the men in black vests firmly stopped in their way, "Joe, Joe Monk!"

"Yes, sir, Mr. Alridge."

"Joe, I have here with me the committee of the North and South, and, young man, there has been a disturbing development, for we have received . . . uncontroverted proof . . . that you are not Joe Monk of Massachusetts but, in fact, are Joe Monk of Olive Chapel, and for that reason, and that reason alone your application to play in this tournament has been based on a fraudulent affirmation; and, we here assembled have the duty, young man, to end this great match in spite in your plan."

"Mr. Alridge, what are you saying. Joe and I played a great match here. Certainly you . . . certainly you gentlemen can't allow this technicality to mar one of golf's greatest performances for I'm surely defeated, short a miracle."

"Mr. Smead, now this is not your concern, you too have played a great match and will be a deserving champion . . ."

"Joe, we have no choice. Our standards . . . ah, our . . . bylaws . . . yes, our bylaws and our rules that must never be broken . . . you know, Joe, golf by its nature is a very unforgiving game, and we must play by the rules, the rules of the North and the South."

"Well, Mr. Alridge, with all respect, golf is a game of honor and respect for all men, and Joe Monk is my friend and my fellow competitor and . . . "

"Mr. Smead, you speak well, you speak like a champion, and you shall be our champion!"

"Mr. Eldridge, with all . . . due . . . respect, I cannot accept your championship; and, in the event Joe Monk is not crowned champion of this tournament, then I shall and I hereby do withdraw in protest."

"Mr. Smead consider your future, there are powerful men in this game of golf and . . ."

"Mr. Eldridge, please say no more, because with every word you speak our great game is diminished, and I shall hear no more of it."

Joe looked stunned, and for the second time that day his knees buckled - as slowly the realization consumed him that this championship, this one event, and not only this - but his future was being comprised and challenged for a dark and sinister reason; and, as his eyes welled with tears, two great hands met on each shoulder and around him as Ross and Smead and the great prodigy walked arm and arm through the crowd, which stood stunned, and shaken, and not a bit proud, of the actions of these black vested men with white vested interests; and, the day was now ended, and so this champion portended, as if with a knife cut off from his future because of his race, and he so walked homeward, to the farm and to grace.

CHAPTER NINE

WE ALL GO HOME

Summer, Two Thousand Ten

"Papa, you don't mean that's the end of it, do you?"

"Well, shortly after my grandfather told me this sad tale my mother came back to Olive Chapel to take me home to prepare for school and the winter and sports, and life in Davidson County, far from Olive Chapel and . . ."

"Well, papa, tell me about Joe, I've got to know more about Joe!"

"We're almost there, see there to the right the old church, Olive Chapel, and just beyond the graveyard where Mr.

Elvis and Miss Pearl and so many others lie, resting from the long hot days with tobacco, and there down the road off to the right - Miss Pearl's childhood home; now by the creek where your grandmother swam and up the hill to the right - there's the dirt road. And they drove slowly that late afternoon, both now speechless as the old house came into view on the left, and they parked by the kitchen where his grandparents always stood to welcome and to wave.

"Let's stop here and get out. I don't see any lights in the house; but, there in the back - do you see that old shed, that's the last place I saw Joe, I hope he's not dead. Let's just walk down the road and see if the low grounds are still there - I know they are. I want you to see where your grandfather spent so many wonderful days behind a mule and a plow and a tobacco sled and where little Joe Monk played . . . I just want you to see it."

As they walked in the late afternoon glow both Olive decedents spoke not a word, but hand in hand they walked and smelled that blessed land, a bit cooler as the road drifted down and then up and then down toward the old tenant house and the tractor road ruts that extended to the low grounds and then the road disappeared and as they approached the precipice - there, a sound was heard and another . . . and another . . .

"Crack! . . crack! . . crack! . ."

"Do you hear that?"

"Yes, Papa."

They walked down the steep embankment as the sun was setting, both knowing that something would happen that they wouldn't be forgetting - for years beyond . . . . . . and there he stood . . . . . . the great black man, now older, yet still strong and broad shouldered and grey-headed and proud.

"Who goes there, sir."

"It's . . ."

"Mr. Jimmy, is that you? Why I thought it was Mr.

Elvis . . . And who is this child . . . looks like your own . . . must be your grandchild . . . and, now you're home!"

"Is that you Joe, I didn't know if you were still alive, but I'm so glad. You just won't believe why I'm here, and I cannot believe that you're here, in the low grounds. I've just told your story, of your golf, and Pinehurst and Watertown and Pinehurst and the North and South."

"Oh, Mr. Jimmy, those were great days, but, the good Lord brought me home when I needed to be home, with my family and not to far off places, each of which would fail in comparison to his sacred land. Did you notice the house, my house on the hill - its painted."

"No, Joe, when I heard the sound, the Crack! I could think of nothing else but you and your majestic swing and that championship match."

"Now . . . how did you know ? . . I know, Mr. Elvis told you, didn't he? Most folks around here long forgot those days, but one day Mr. Elvis told me that he would make sure that what happened in my life would never be forgotten; and, I begged him to leave it alone, but he was a proud and a good man who loved us black folks like his own. Do you know Mr. Jimmy, when he heard what happened, he cried . . . he just took off his wire glasses and put his white hair in his hands and sobbed, and he and Miss Pearl let me stay up there in the big house until I recovered from the shock of what had happened. Now I don't want to make too much of it, but, it was my own fault, I let my life go down hill and took up with drinking, anything I could find, and my life was just a mess, but then some time in the fifties Miss Pearl made me get help; and, you're not going to believe this but now I'm glad it all worked out that way because nothing could ever come close to the life I've had here."

"You mean . . . you mean you've been perfectly content here?"

"Oh, yes - I'm no different from anyone else who loves the game. We all want to live our lives 'out there' - we think - viving for championships; but most can't - they have jobs, and - I had mine - for I'm really a farmer and as such have lived far better than most. I'm not one bit different from all other golfers, for all golfers have a championship swing tucked deep down inside - it's getting it out that's the challenge; but, everyone has it, I'm convinced of that - and mine was not better or worse - it just came out sooner. I'm convinced that all golfers sooner or later, with persistence and play and experimentation and fortitude can unlock their great swing - as I did mine. Oh, don't pity me, 'cause I'm like you - I love the game and have experienced it more fully here in the low grounds than at Oakmount or your country club - 'cause it's mainly in the mind when it's fun; it's the search and the quest - not the championship stress, that makes golf a game, that's not the same, as all the rest."

"But Joe, did you . . ."

"Did Mr. Elvis tell you about - - Savannah?"

"What a beautiful story, I know you miss her."

"Yes, sir, but while I decided that I would give up championship golf, I didn't want to give up Savannah. After Miss Pearl helped me get things all straightened out, after we sold the crop in fifty one, you know how Mr. Elvis would let each of us have three acres as our own; well, I got right back on that Greyhound at New Hill and headed up Highway 1 to the North, not knowing if she'd still be there and not knowing what I was going to do or what I was going to say or where I was going to live. The game taught me to win and to lose but in both to be a fighter and to take chances, to risk disappointment in search of great joy.

"Boston and Watertown and Cambridge were beautiful in May when I arrived. I walked the three miles from Cambridge to Harvard Square, slowing down the nearer I got, and I just walked around the Yard for several hours before getting the courage to go to her store. I didn't know whether she was married, had moved off, had kids, but I decided to hit a one iron to a pin set deep over a high lipped bunker instead of the safe two to the front of the green; and, when I walked in that store - - it was different, but it was the same, and as she looked up and as our eyes met the ball bounced once to the right and settled three feet below the hole, and I knew my gamble had paid off.

"Well, she closed up the store right then, and we walked down to the river. I rented a girling boat, and we floated out into the dark river and planned our future; and, I just held her, and she held me until all the lights in all the buildings of that great university went out.

"The next morning she insisted on a long walk, to the west, down by the Longfellow house - on down Mount Auburn Street toward Watertown; and, then she took me up through that great cemetery - and she wouldn't tell me why - but, then we walked up a slope that overlooked the river, the town and the city. She walked slowly toward a stone, one like I'd never seen - for it was black granite and white granite all intermixed - it stood out and was the most beautiful. She knelt - and I knelt and she pointed her fingers to the grooves that read "O'RIELY, MAGGIE KELLY" . . . and under her name - the inscription . . . "BELOVED MOTHER OF THREE DAUGHTERS AND ONE SON." And my heart broke because my mamma had not forgotten me. Savannah then told me that she had done some asking and reading and had discovered that to those in Boston, Maggie Kelly had been known as the mother of three girls, but, in her will, her last request was for that tombstone, and that inscription, and all who knew her thought the boy must have been a stillborn . . . but . . . he wasn't . . .

"Savannah and I embraced and sat there leaning against the stone, and we talked of my mother, and we talked of our future, and we decided to go back home and to live the good life above the low grounds, not that far from where my mother and father first fell in love - in Pinehurst, just south of Olive Chapel.

From that day forward, I never felt lonely again because I knew my mother loved me, and I knew of her sacrifice, and I knew that Savannah and I together on the farm was better than being the greatest gulfer because I have the greatest life a man could have."

"Wow, Mr. Joe, but do you ever play . . ."

"Joe, I've been worried about you all my life, not knowing what happened to you, and now I can rest easy too. Joe, do you mind me asking - all these years, do you still think about the game, have you watched, well do you watch . . . you had the great Curtis Smead on the ropes."

"Well, we had a great match, and I've loved his success, and the people have loved him 'cause he's a man of principal, a friendly man, and he's been a great champion."

"Joe, I had an unusual experience last year, was asked to be at an occasion with , and we even had time to talk for a while. One thing led to another, my love for Pinehurst and Wake Forest and all that; and, he stopped me and insisted on telling me about the greatest black golfer he'd ever known and then he said, 'No the greatest golfer I've ever known, and his name was Joe Monk.' One thing led to another. Of course the name rang a bell, and he insisted on me doing something, and I promised him I would - I promised him that I would come back to Olive Chapel and see if you were here and if you were to tell you this . . . ah . . . Joe, he wants you to have a green jacket, his very own first Master's jacket . . . because he told me, that without your match he could never have survived the pressure, that if you'd have played on, that you would have been so much better than anyone else, that he wouldn't have earned it in the first place."

"Why, why, I just don't . . ."

"Joe, this is one of those times when you can't say no. He needs to do this, this is something you can do for him as much as something he can do for you."

"Mr. Joe?"

"Mr. Joe, about that ninth lesson, do you think it would work for me?"

"Joe, would you do one thing for me, would you show us your swing?"

"Well, sir, I told Mr. Elvis when I came home that no white man would ever see my swing again, but there were three people excluded from that pledge, Mr. Elvis, Mr. Elvis' grandson, and his grandchild . . . so let me go find my stick and, youngster, over yonda find me the shiniest white rock you can; and, look up into the sky and let me know when a crow comes over those trees out over the low grounds for my vision is not what it was, and they get up on me a bit too fast."

And with that, the prodigy, his hands still strong though slightly twisted, wrapped his long tentacles around the end of his well worn tobacco stick and then . . .

"Mr. Joe, there I see him! There comes one."

The prodigy turned and lined up to the descending sun, set his right hip firmly and his head as if in a cast, and he squeezed his grip tightly and set his right elbow low and inside, the look of the "K" was now set and well established and the key was in place and the backswing still full but not quite as far with the hands stretched upwards with hardly a jar of those hips that were set now, his torso all twisted like a spring fully loaded, he let loose in reaction which, with the force of his legs and the power all connected, with a Crack! the rock exploded ever heavenward and beyond it rose toward that crow like a meteor from beyond, and it soared and disappeared in the light of the sun as it set ore the low grounds, his tournament now won; and, the look of utter satisfaction and pleasure on Joe

Monk's face - only a golfer can know, in his soul, the purity of the motion, raptured from God's gift of flow - reactive clubhead speed - squarely applied to an object - propelling it to orbit - to a sight intended - completion.

EPILOGUE

"THE STORY BEHIND THE STORY"

The <u>Saga of Joe Monk</u> is based on existing places and people who lived, are living and who hopefully will live. Circumstances of the author's life came to bear in most interesting ways and, to him, in ways that not only were intriguing but in some instances quite amazing. Because of my affection for Olive Chapel, the Elvis Elisha Olive Family, Wake Forest, the Brown Family of Boston, Joe Monk and those like him and golf, this saga has been a fulfilling and thrilling joy to pen.

In the mid 1950's I would be in the company of my mother's parents, Pearl and Elvis Olive in Olive Chapel, sometimes with my sister, Jean Olive, and sometimes alone. These were summer visits to Papa's and Grandmommie's sprawling tobacco farm in eastern Wake County in east central North Carolina. These were days that would make any city boy's heart flutter: awakening to the sound at daybreak of a tractor engine starting, hearing the hoofbeats of mules pulling tobacco sleds, smelling ham and eggs and biscuits sizzling and baking in that small cozy kitchen and feeling the cool breezes rustle the curtains of the upstairs window of the old farm house, surrounded on all sides by the contiguous farms of our relatives, the Olives and the Goodwins. After breakfast we would pick up the many tenant farmers, all of whom were African-American, to perform our daily tasks. It was late on one of those days while standing in the dirt road between the house and milk barn that I heard my grandmother announce that Joe Monk had again drunk perfume; and, from the other side and from within the milkhouse my uncle replied that it might well be time for him to die. (I would add here that those words were not intended to be cruel and were spoken by one of the finest people I have ever known. They were words of exasperation and words of fact that all that could be done had been done.) For whatever reason that occurrence has remained in my mind and, of late, a gnawing purpose developed within me to give Joe Monk his due and in doing so to write about the places and things which have brought such warmth and joy to my life.

My early history was interspersed with ballgames at Old Wake Forest, the alma mater of my father, his brother and many of those of the Snyder family. Wake Forest was the college choice for southern Baptist young men with little means but with great motivation. It was and has remained a bastion for free and independent thought and from that sleepy eastern Carolina village has risen to its current lofty heights academically and athletically.

The Olive Chapel community does lie along U.S. Highway 1 and is surrounded by Old Wake Forest to the north, Chapel Hill to the west, New Hill to the east and the incomparable Pinehurst area to the south. Highway 1 in fact does link the Olive Chapel area to Boston and Watertown and Oakley farther to the north and to Augusta farther to the south. The manuscript was completed without my ever determining that Augusta was along U.S. Highway 1, and then I checked, and it was, and I was not surprised.

102

The Watertown, Oakley connection originates from my daughter having married Kevin Mitchell Brown who was the Massachusetts high school golf champion who played and caddied at Oakley Country Club and who, with his family, introduced me to that beautiful area. In fact James Tufts was a member at Oakley, did create Pinehurst and did bring with him the pro at Oakley, Donald Ross, to live and create him masterpiece, Pinehurst Number 2. The North and South Amateur and Open were the preeminent southern spring tournaments preceding the Masters and the Amateur continues to be one of the two or three leading amateur tournaments in America.

From those roots a seed was planted which lay dormant until my friend Roger S. Tripp, an attorney in Lexington, introduced me to a great book, <u>The Legend of Bagger Vance</u>.

Several months later I sat with my family in our church and enjoyed our favorite service "The Nine Lessons and Carols," a beautiful series of stories and songs presented the Sunday before Christmas. My second greatest sin is sitting in church fiddling with my hands attempting to create new and better golf grips. My first greatest sin tends to be continually manipulating my golf game and swing with results which renownly have been negative. Yet golf has been a special part of my life as have the many tinkerings with my swing, grip, stance and golf philosophy. Every two weeks I tend to jot down and stuff into my billfold eight or nine swing keys, the results of which precisely for a day and a half convince me that the Masters is within my reach - only for these swing keys to fail, leading to more experimentation and more swing keys. Well, back to church - it was at the pre-Christmas service that the thought occurred, ah-ha, "The Nine Lessons and Carols" - "The Nine Lessons of Golf:" Joe Monk and his saga would be about his life and struggles and nine secrets which were made known to him or discovered by him in his quest to fulfill a natural talent which was even mythical.

Not much more was thought about the subject until later that night in the shower. It was under the "hot water" that my mind practically exploded with the interconnection of geography and personalities, with my desire to put on the map Olive Chapel and at the same time to respond to my deeply seeded desire to breath life and respect into this forgotten man and at the same time to talk about a game of which I know so little.

My wife knew I was up to something the way I bolted from the shower and feverishly searched for paper (there is never writing paper in a lawyer's house). I found a small yellow notebook with my wife's notes of and about our daughter's wedding. Within an hour the saga of Joe Monk in outline form and of necessary chapters flowed onto that yellow paper. When finished I stopped and knew without thinking and without planning how many chapters had been outlined. I counted the number and the number was nine, a number which would correspond perfectly with the nine lessons of golf. Oftentimes I have gone back to attempt to recreate the sequence of events of this book and at no time have I been able to justify changing the original nine chapters which flowed so effortlessly late that Sunday night.

There followed more "fill in" notes roughly inserted in and around these nine chapters. But, there was a missing link: I needed to return to Boston and Watertown to revisit Oakley, Belmont, Bedford, Sudbury, Waltham, Weston and even Quincy Market, Faneuil Hall, the Boston Commons, and most important of all, Harvard Square. So as a weekend excursion, our daughter Courtney and Kevin, her husband, and my wife, Sandra, and I returned to Boston to explore golf and to visit the Browns. My wife and I stayed at the Inn at Harvard Square which overlooks Harvard Yard, enough to inspire any writer. Just exploring the campus, the libraries, both legal and general, touring the Longfellow house, all on a previous trip, had wetted my appetite to return.

On the first morning a series of interesting events caught my attention. After a pleasing breakfast at Au Bon Pain, my wife and I turned up an alley behind the Harvard Coop and there in graffiti on the back door was written "Monk Hate." My wife and I stopped in wonderment because the name "Monk" is not common. We proceeded around through the alleyway and there on another door in graffiti was the expletive "Monk M... F..." Around the next corner was a bookstore, Savannah Books. It was small yet for some reason I felt it necessary to go in and look around. The door appeared to be locked. We came out and went back and tried again and entered this small bookstore which was in fact entirely stocked with books about black people and by black writers. I didn't realize any connection until my eye caught several books which were necessary and perfect as a part of my research. The waitress in that bookstore was a beautiful young lady of mixed culture who would later become Savanna Book and who would be described as Joe Monk's girlfriend. Then being quite thrilled and amazed with my find, we proceeded back to the lovely sitting area of the Inn at Harvard Square. While my wife was resting, I went over to the expansive library area in the lobby, and the first book I noticed was a book of Falkner's novels written between the years 1942 and 1953 which contained much of Afro American lore. (The original idea for any novel I would write was derived from the reading of a faux Falkner contest in an airline magazine while flying some years before.) Now here in my hand was the last piece of the puzzle, discovered while on a research tour, Falkner's own work and style from which I would be edified.

Later that day, by the way, I asked the hotel receptionist if that book could be purchased there and she said "No, but you can purchase it at the Harvard Coop." We then returned to the

Coop and purchased that book. Please recall that on the back of the Coop was inscribed the graffiti about "Monk Hate."

Later that day we were taken by Dorothy Jean Brown, Kevin's mother, to Redbones Barbecue just around the corner from Tip O'Neil's homeplace. There in the back of that barbecue I would see images of Joe Monk working with the many wonderful people there.

The following day Ed and Beverly Brown guided us to a thrilling experience, dinner at the Wayside Inn. The Wayside Inn is part of American history and is in Sudbury. It once was purchased by Henry Ford for restoration purposes and now is best known for its connection with Longfellow. (On our last trip to Boston we had toured the Longfellow house and had learned of the tragic death of his wife when her dress caught fire.) It was to the front room of the Wayside Inn that Longfellow came when he had developed writer's block after the death of his wife and there was inspired to write The Tales of the Wayside Inn, the beginning lines being "Listen my children and you shall hear of the midnight ride of Paul Revere . . ." I made mention of this event and the Falkner book in no way to make comparisons but simply to indicate how thrilling these coincidences were. It indeed would be foolish to make too much of meaningless coincidences in our lives; however, it doesn't hurt to have open minds and hearts to opportunities and occurrences of inspiration.

Well, after all this, what do Joe Monk, Olive Chapel, Wake Forest, Pinehurst, Watertown, Donald Ross, Savannah Books, good country fried chicken, a six iron perfectly struck to a target intended, have in common? Each are tucked way down deeply within me, as in each are tucked way down deeply those things which have made life smooth and warm and human. The true purpose of The Saga of Joe Monk is the regurgitation of an appreciation for that spirit because it binds us with things living and all things spiritual; because we are not separate from anything; and it is at those points of connection and the interrelationships of objects and places and people and thoughts and games and accomplishments and failures that total a sum, and that sum is the essence of existence because it is who we are - and by writing it down it becomes more realized and permanent.

Oh, by the way, the author has in his attic a classic 1952 Spalding Top-Flite Synchro-Dyne five iron, the face of which is as the surface of the moon, all pitted with indentations of many pebbles struck while walking along Carolina's dirt roads and planning and thinking about Mr. Ross's great game.